CLAIRVIOLENCE
TALES OF TAROT AND TORMENT

MO MOSHATY

Cover art by Bri Crozier
Interior Illustrations by
Mo Moshaty & Matt Blairstone
Edited by Alex Woodroe

Content warnings are available at the end of this book. Please consult this list for any particular subject matter you may be sensitive to.

TENEBROUS PRESS

Selected Works from Tenebrous Press:

Reef Mind
a novella by Hazel Zorn

We Like it Cherry
a novel by Jacy Morris

Puppet's Banquet
by Valkyrie Loughcrewe

Casual
a novel by Koji A. Dae

All Your Friends are Here
stories by M.Shaw

TRVE CVLT
a novel by Michael Bettendorf

A Spectre is Haunting Greentree
a novel by Carson Winter

From the Belly
a novel by Emmett Nahil

Brave New Weird: The Best New Weird Horror (+More)
Three volumes, various, edited by Alex Woodroe

In Somnio: A Collection of Modern Gothic Horror
Various, edited by Alex Woodroe

Green Inferno: The World Celebrates Your Demise
Various, edited by Matt Blairstone

More titles at www.TenebrousPress.com

READING THE CARDS

The Card
The Tale

For Andrew—thank you for being my light in the dark, and my anchor in the roughest of storms.

THE DEVIL

THE FEVER MAN

DECEMBER OF '08 was off to a good start. The house we'd dreamed of was ours at a steal and I'd be celebrating my third year at The Potter Query—Vanderbilt's First-Class New Journal, making me Jim Purdy, head writer. It was about time.

Pam left her vet job and was expecting, and folks were happy that we'd finally done something worthy of our large families. Pam was the second eldest of twelve, and me, the baby of seven. We had reluctantly decided on Mortimer for a boy, mostly due to the bullshit story she said my grandfather laid on her about my great-grandfather Mort finding some abandoned baby deer in the woods and nursing it back to full pulsing vitality before releasing it back into the wild.

Truth be told, my great-grandfather Mort was a drunk who used to shoot at cans most of the day while my great-grandmother would bake dozens of pies at once and sell them each day in town. This 'prized deer' was no more than a kitten he'd almost stepped on while taking a walk and he had left the poor creature in someone's mailbox. I was praying for a Junie, after my late mother. She had decided to get out while the getting was good. Breast cancer. She was diagnosed on a Thursday and, no one to fuss about when the bad news came, was dead by Wednesday.

We'd had it all laid out, starting a family in our early thirties. It was one of those times where 'waiting until we were financially stable to have kids' panned out without much counter-fanfare. A larger home to grow into, 401(k)s, good insurance. "Daisy", my mother used to say, when everything was to a 'T.'

Pam's bleeding started at 4:07 pm on the first Tuesday of January, just a bit. The doctor told Pam not to worry but in our usual fashion, Pam and I were already sitting in the hospital parking lot, just to be sure. Pam was silent, eyes closed. She wasn't one for jokes at the moment and I tried to cut the air often for levity. She waved her hand in my direction, and I knew.

Shut the fuck up for once, Jim.

'I think I have to use the bathroom. Wait here.' Pam opened the car door and winced as she stood; she blanched at the driver's seat, dark red with blood.

I hopped out and swung around the car to cradle her from stumbling and we raced to the emergency entrance. A sea of medicinal green coats and scrubs flew around us like a flock of birds descending on dinner scraps, screaming questions that Pam was too bereft to answer. I tried to focus on one question at a time. I remember losing my temper often and feeling very apologetic. My eyes met Pam's and for a split second, she wasn't mine. She was someone's daughter, someone's friend going through a terrible time, a woman in a film about facing adversity.

I could only watch to see how the ending played out. Sit and watch. Pam went into labor within the hour. Two hours and nineteen minutes later, the doctor came out to tell us our daughter was dead—my little Junie. Pam was reassured that there was no reason why she wouldn't make an astounding recovery, and we could try again within the year if we wanted.

As I looked up hazy-eyed, a thin grey blob moved out from behind the doctor. It circled around to come right in front of me. I rubbed my eyes, and it was gone. Stress. Pam was despondent for the next two days. On our second night at the hospital, she broke her silence.

'You named her Junie. I like that.'

'It fits.'

'I knew she wouldn't make it. Months ago. When I had the flu.' Pam looked out the hospital window at nothing at all.

'What do you mean? Did you tell your doctor?' I had to take the anger out of my voice as I was hearing this distressing news for the first time. I mindfully softened my mouth.

'No. She was healthy up until then. Up until the dreams started.'

I edged around the bed slowly, so as not to startle her. I wanted to rush her badly, crush her into me. Take all the sadness away.

Wearily, she turned her head toward me, and I had to nail

myself to the floor to not react. Her lips matched her skin, and all the beautiful Highland green with the vibrant orange flecks had been pulled from her eyes and replaced with a filthy seafoam.

'Pam, talk to me,' I said. I grasped her hand and followed it up the wrist and watched her skin goose pimple at my touch. Icebox hands, she'd tell me, when I'd reach to hold her in the night. I instinctively apologized but she didn't recoil this time. Just laid there, watching nothing.

'He stands in the yard,' she said.

'Who?'

'The man in my dream. Every time is the same. I start the seedlings in the shed. I water them and grab the flats to stick in the greenhouse. And he's there.' Pam straightened and sat up on one elbow. I reached out to steady her.

'What did he look like?' I asked.

'Like nothing?'

'Nothing?' Pulling the anger out of my voice was getting harder. Fuck's sake, pull yourself together, man.

'Like nothing, static, I don't know. You could see through him, but he was darker somehow, like a shadow. Just standing there, like a liquid in the middle of the yard between the shed and the house. I would walk to the left, and he would move there too. Then I would go right, and he would move too. Just wouldn't let me pass.'

'That's terrible.' My mouth was horrifically dry, and that was all I could muster.

'And then I'd wake up and I'd have this weird sort of haze at the corner of my eye and then I'd close my eyes, and it'd go away. Just like that. Every night.'

'Like a grey blob?'

Her eyes widened in panic, and she turned her head quickly back to the hospital window and watched the light drops of rain that kissed the glass.

Sitting silently, I thought about how in the hell we would explain this to people. And then I thought, fuck 'em, who cares. I thought about helping Pam break down the nursery. Or keeping it up and trying again. I thought about how many times we might go through this in the future. Keeping house for a baby that might never join it. I thought about Pam and her broken heart and seafoam eyes that looked like they were searching for something.

It would take another three hours for us to speak again.

Pam told me how the dreams escalated, this Fever Man of sorts would start playing a mocking game of shadowing her, chasing her, clutching her, and, as of last night, eating her. Then his shadow darkened and began to color itself until it was a fully physical man. With brute strength and missing eyes and a mouth wider than his head, adorned with a million nail-like teeth.

'I'm going to take it away, he'd say.' She sighed heavily. 'I always thought he meant my life.' Pam cried. She tightened her grip on my hand until her knuckles whitened.

It was sleeting now, and it made a slapping noise that agitated me; slapping me awake to notice that the world keeps turning even in death. Even in nightmares. Pam hadn't eaten or drank since arriving. I'd gotten her to eat two ice chips in the night. Her temperature was slowly coming down, which relieved her nurse. Her goose pimples had gone away, and I watched her eyes grow heavy. And shut. And stay that way.

I allowed my head to hang, just for a bit. It didn't take long for sleep to come. Twenty-six. The number of words my wife would speak to me that last day in the hospital. I wondered where her mind went, where it explored as she drifted off in the middle of sentences. Today, we would be leaving Valley Oaks Community Hospital's Maternity Ward; the cordoned-off wing for mothers with extreme cases like preeclampsia or severe gestational diabetes or loss. The walls were a lovely shade of blue-grey, peaceful. I'd noticed the room was delicate, quaint, and with no sign of a baby animal or suggestion of a child anywhere. No bassinet corner or rattle border on the wall. Nothing to make you remember what you wouldn't be carrying home. Thank Christ I hadn't put the car seat in the Jeep yet. Pam stumbled a bit getting into the wheelchair and indignantly yelled at the attending nurse to get the hell out of the way. The nurse's eyes shot down to the floor in an 'it's okay, I get it.' But how could she?

My wife's eyes, once the dreamiest damn shade of green, faded into the scratchy hue of a worn wooden fence. Cold. Pupils like pin dots. It occurred to me that I was not only leaving without our daughter in tow, but I was leaving behind a large piece of what sprung my partner to life as well, tangled somewhere within the cheap and cooling sheets of that hospital bed. She was defeated, ashamed, and angry. And it would take a good month for Pam's eyes to come around to the green that I knew.

Pam and I decided to try once more in the Spring, but we did not.

The winter drew in fast this year. We'd already been scraping ice off our cars since October, so sitting close together, reading while a fire roared, was our happy place over the months. The snow was beating harder than a whip that day. We'd kept the baby's room the same. The unused 'Baby's First Christmas' ornament still tucked neatly in the tissue paper on the right-hand side of the top dresser drawer. The room was a world untouched by prying eyes, eyes that gazed at the floor and met with mouths that twisted in an 'it's a shame' gesture. Door closed.

Within this 'cozy time,' as Pam called it, we giggled as she circled inspirational outfits out of the Vicky's Secret catalog. Lacy things weren't usually her thing, but I wondered if she felt she needed them now. For what reason I'll never know. She seemed hopeful and happy skimming and circling. I didn't want to interrupt by saying that the old oversized purple t-shirt that hung off her shoulder still made me randy as all get out. When she volunteered for Camp Good Days and Special Times, they gave her a 3x volunteer t-shirt by mistake. But she wore it proudly anyway, and God did I love that.

But who can say that at a time like this? 'Oh babe, just put on the shirt from the dying kids camp, that turns me on.' Not hardly.

A sharp cough broke her laughter. She'd been looking a bit peaked in the last weeks, and she'd mentioned a tickle in her throat and a bit of congestion that came and went every New England winter since she'd been a child. Ethel, she called it, the first flu of the winter. She'd get two more before the last frost. This time Ethel sat rumbling in her chest like a thundercloud. She hacked turning red, gasping. She flung her legs out of the shared blanket and tried to stand, holding her arms above her head, she gazed at me, eyes wide, the green fading again. I clasped my hands around her waist and looked her deep in the eyes.

'Slow, honey, slow.' She gasped, followed by a controlled exhale, and wheezed slightly back in.

'Good. Good. Now try to breathe deeply.' Her eyes fell and sunk into her skull leaving a greyish ring behind. Her cheeks lost their rosy pink that bloomed within them as she circled.

'I think,' she wheezed, 'I better lie down.'

'Yeah, you're not looking so tough, champ.' She shot me an annoyed glance and then smiled weakly.

As if that was my cue, I picked her up gently and carried her into the bedroom we'd taken on the first floor. Pam couldn't bear being across the room from an empty nursery, who could blame her, so I moved everything in an afternoon while Pam went shopping. Even grabbed that expensive bedding she had her heart set on. I could feel her eyes watching me as I lumbered slowly into the bedroom. Pam was a whip of a woman but leaning over a desk ten hours a day trying to find something worthwhile to write made my spine feel seventy at best. In that blended moment of her gaze meeting my cheek, me stepping over the threshold of the bedroom and side-glancing at her sad, sick face, a moment of terror struck me. Pam's eyes widened more than I'd ever seen them. She stared straight into my office doorway and began to scream. Without as much as a glance in that direction, I began to scream too, and my knees almost buckled as Pam thrashed violently. It took all my strength to pull her up from falling clean to the floor. My back pinched.

'What?!' I found myself shouting through gritted teeth and felt the guilt wash over me.

'Do you see it?!' she panted.

'See what?' My eyes darted around.

'The office! Look!' I stared keenly, squinting my eyes like that could somehow help, having less line of vision. Nothing.

I hoisted her higher onto my chest and looked again. Nothing, until—

A scant outline of something holding firm within my office, something clear, faint. And then it moved to the right, out of sight, and we both screamed, terrified at what seemed to be the edge of a thick grey blob. I rushed into the bedroom, dropping Pam harder than I wanted to, and she shoo-ed me away, understanding. She pulled her knees into her chest, wheezing. I darted back into the hallway. Square with my office door.

'Please, Jim, don't! Come back!' She coughed loudly, a bark. 'Jim!'

You see it in movies, where the world turns out of focus behind the main actor in those tense, will they-won't they situations that make you cling to your seat. Will he meet the killer head-on? Will he push at the moving curtain though there's nothing there? Is the killer behind him? I stepped further into the hallway, four feet from the door. Almost begging it to come back into view. A small whistling noise pinged in my ears, slow and rhythmic at first, and then a tea kettle blast at once. It was Pam, hollering from the bedroom doorway, clinging to the frame.

'Jim, please, come back!' Her face was streaked with tears and the ruddiness had come back with a vengeance.

It wasn't the best-case scenario for pumping the circulation back into a man's ill wife's face, but I'd take it. She was screaming because I'd carelessly ambled into the middle of my office. I ran out, darting my head back in to check out the space which, on deep ocular discovery, was empty. No outline, no blob, nothing but wooden paneling and those red and beige checkered curtains all country homes are supposed to own, no questions asked.

I rushed back to the bedroom and scrambled Pam toward the bed. Flinging the sheets back I tucked her in quickly and then sat. I was breathless, panting almost. Her eyes held so much confusion and horror. It had come back, this dream figure, this blob. I patted Pam's head, damp and burning.

'Oh babe, you're burning up.'

She clutched my wrist tightly, pulling it into her.

'You saw it?'

'I did.'

'He's real. From my dream, but he's real.'

'I think we might have a ghost, maybe?' I was as sure of my words as a bumbling American tourist. A ghost? What the hell was I saying? I couldn't give her any comfort. I couldn't tell her she was hallucinating; I couldn't tell her she was just seeing things; she had a fever.

'My God that's it. Pam.'

'What? What's it? Jim, what?

'You have a fever. It came the last time you had a fever.'

'But I have nothing left for him to take. He took our daughter, took her right from us.' Pam sobbed weakly, her wheezing breaking its hum. I clutched her tight to me and rocked her.

We sat in silence for almost an hour. Pulling back, I pushed the wet hair off her forehead and kissed it. Hot, still.

'Make me a coma. One of those TheraFlu thingies.'

'Oh, good idea.' She looked drowsy and fought it with her flickering eyes.

As I headed to the kitchen, I couldn't help but glance in the direction of my office. Nothing. I can't remember how long I'd stared at the 'Home Sweet Heaven' wood-carved lumber piece that hung over the kitchen windows before the whistling jolted me so fast my mouth yelped an actual 'Yarr!' This time it was only the tea kettle squealing its highest soprano pitch. I dug around the old red bread box that houses various medicinal things like aspirin, several bottles of expired vitamins Pam and I always forgot to take regularly, unfinished prescriptions, and cold and flu meds. I poured the sickly lime-colored powder into the mug and shot a quick splash of hot water to mix first. Pam always said if you did it in one shot it got grainy and all yuck at the bottom. I listen well. I stirred the rest of the water in the mug when a pop startled me. It was quickly followed by a long hiss.

I crept out of the kitchen to a quiet hallway. Pam had stopped coughing. I stood at the bedroom door watching her and her low buzz of a snore. Out of the corner of my eye, I saw something in my office doorway move. I darted left quickly, spilling the piping hot coma all over my hand and dropping the mug in a crash. 'Fuck!' I shouted, shaking my left hand viciously, watching the red skin bubble up. I shot over to Pam, still snoring except the snore had taken on a weird hum. Hum, buzz, hum, hum, hum, buzz, hum, hum. Then faster. Humbuzzhumhum, humbuzzhumhum. Faster still. As I listened, I began to realize she was laughing. In her dead sleep, laughing. Her lips curled sharply at the corners and the noise grew by decibels. The laugh was maniacal, rhythmic.

'Pam? Pam, baby?' I walked slowly backward, startled as my shoulders hit the opposite wall of the hallway. I let my vision drift back to the office doorway.

The blob had returned and structured itself to the loose shape of a man. Part of me wanted to laugh as his stance was a bit like Yosemite Sam, all bow-legged and hunched forward at the waist. But any thought of fleeting amusement ceased as I followed the figure upwards and caught its gaping hole of what could only be something of a mouth congested with thousands of razor-sharp teeth. The din of Pam's laugh took over the room and spilled into the hallway. Her head had turned unnaturally towards me, and her eyes were wide and glassy. The dirty seafoam had been replaced with milky white sacs that seemed too large to fit in the spaces they'd been put. Her mouth hung painfully loose and screamed its humming buzzsaw of laughter as her body undulated under the covers. I winced at the pain she must have been in, in this fever dream, this Fever Man taking over us. I pushed off the wall, my hand stinging wildly from the pain and stepped toward the bedroom door.

'Pam! Pam stop it!'

A bang filled the house. Most of the wall décor dropped off the living room walls near the office. The bedroom door slammed, and the laughing stopped. I reached for the doorknob but was stopped by the scorching heat of a mouth-shaped hole held by a man who was no longer loose-shaped but very, very solid, very, very real, and very, very close. A million prickles of teeth grazed my face like the ping of a hard Spring sleet. Something warm and wet trickled down my neck, first in slow, long droplets and then a steady stream. I tried to pull against the teeth, but they only ripped further into my neck. This thing, this man, was swallowing me whole. And I wasn't fearful, you see, but quite the opposite. More forlorn, trusting. This monster pulled me further into him, easing me gently down whatever throat he may have. And all I could do was let him take me down, down, into the black. I thought of what Pam might think when she finally awoke. Would she see me lying there, drenched in some sort of grease or just see shards of a man put through the ringer? Presented like a regurgitated cat prize. Would she even wake up? Was she even my wife anymore?

A woman who not more than two hours ago sat grinning, circling pieces of inspiring lingerie for our next celebratory romp to prospective parenthood. Was she even alive? I sat in the black for what seemed like ages, or hours, I couldn't be sure. Seated or standing or lying in the fetal position, I couldn't be sure of that either. A complete absence of senses should have been sending me into panic, but I'd never felt more clarity and calmness in all my life.

I patted myself, feeling around for the usual things like my wallet, phone, and body. Nothing. Was I just two eyes peering into the abyss? A ghost in the house. Jim, you pathetic shitbag. What hit me then was my absolute uselessness to Pam. My lack of understanding, or help in a state of panic, of watching her carrying the weight of losing our daughter, just watching her suffer like a bystander at a wreck. Or not being able to get her a damn mug of coma without letting a monster tear us both apart.

I don't remember feeling more alone. I don't even remember waking up this morning or going to sleep last night. Is it all leaving me? I don't remember seeing the world outside of my office window. Or driving home from the hospital. Or getting to the hospital, or getting Pam pregnant, or making love to Pam. I don't remember meeting her family or her meeting mine. Our first date, our second date. Buying this house or talking to a realtor. Talking. Talking to anyone.

Surely I'm not losing my mind.

But here I stand within a blob beast that followed us home from the hospital I never went to or at least can't remember even leaving. I can't even think far enough back beyond the morning of the miscarriage. The miscarriage. Where it all truly began to go black.

A pinhole shot through the darkness and a small dot of light hit me. The hole became wider and wider still, and as the hole crept its way to a tunnel, a rush of tightness caught my chest.

A flutter tickled my abdomen; I was quite sure I'd pissed my shorts. I stared, blinking past the bright whiteness, feeling a sudden rush of pain and panic. Pam emerged from the bedroom, looking drowsy. She stopped suddenly at the puddle of coma, or ghastly spit from the Fever Man—perhaps a mix. She stumbled into the frame of the bedroom door and my body, or what was left, instinctively pulled towards her. But nothing. I couldn't move. I couldn't shout. Could she see me? Hear me? She traveled slowly into the kitchen and disappeared only to reappear looking forlorn. Her eyes searched the great room, her furrowed brow burdened with trouble. She finally set her eyes in my direction and fell slowly to her knees in tears.

Oh, my Pam. Pamela Denise Purdy. I love you. The way I love you right now is ten times more than yesterday. That awful song, I know. But please believe me. Please believe it's true because I beg of you, it is. But I don't remember even marrying you. Kissing your lips for the first time. I don't remember you even leaving for that Camp Good Days event or even being without you one moment. I don't remember. Why don't I remember?

Pam stood and walked over to me. I couldn't reach for her. My Pammy. I'm so sorry. I'm sorry I couldn't save you from this Fever Man. He's taken me in your place and maybe that's enough.

'Jim?'

'Yes, love,' I mumbled from what used to be my mouth, I suppose.

'I'm so sorry Jim. I'm so sorry. I loved you best. Know that. But you had to go, like the rest. You had to. God Jim, I'm so sorry.'

'Pam?'

The rest? I didn't know what I've done or what's been done. Or undone. My brain was hazy and the tunnel to my Pammy grew smaller. And there was nothing I could do or say, or want, or change. Just fade. Just go. A pinhole of seafoam green and I saw my last.

The click-click of a computer keyboard snapped Pam out of a daydream. She watched the fingers of the nurse in purple scrubs. The soft rhythm of the pouncing on keys brought a hum out of Pam.

'Baby Come Back.' The nurse said.

'Huh?' Pam said.

'You were humming 'Baby Come Back,' I love that song.'

Pam sniffed back, lost in thought. 'Oh, yes. It's nice.'

'How are we feeling after the cyst rupture? We're a month out. Pretty severe. You've had an appointment with Doctor Morris last week, it looks like?'

'I'm doing okay, just very tired. And yes, Doctor Morris.'

'That's good to hear, Pam. And the Clozapine?'

'Doing all right. Is the Doctor going to be in soon? I'd really rather discuss things with him.'

'Oh, no problem, I'll snag him.'

Pam's legs dangled off the patient table, and she gazed out at the snowy world from the second-story window of the medical building adorned with red and beige buffalo check curtains. A small, rumbled cough stirred in her chest, and she stifled it. 'Not now, Ethel.' Her cheeks puffed out, eyes watered. The door slowly opened. 'Knock, knock.' The doctor stepped in slowly and Pam's lips parted in a sob.

'Oh dear,' he said. He reached for the Kleenex box and brought it to her. 'What seems to be up, Pam?'

'Oh nothing, I just, I think the therapies and meds are working quite well, doctor.'

'Well, that's good news, right? Why the tears?'

'I've lost Jim, and I loved him best.' Pam dropped her Kleenex and began using the collar of her shirt. The doctor sighed heavily, a marked concern in his eyes. He stepped closer to Pam.

'Well, we knew there'd be focused loss in multiple personalities. I know you relied heavily on Jim; he became your caretaker. But remember, Pam, you can do everything he was doing.'

Pam looks up defiantly. 'I didn't want to lose him. Not like this.'

'Pam, we did say we were going to take it all away, slowly. I'm sorry he had to go. But things were progressing in a way we didn't like. You were creating separate lives, timelines.' He sighed again and took a step backward. 'Pregnancies.'

Pam's spine straightened, then softened, and her nose began to run. The doctor brought the Kleenex back into her view.

'Isn't this what you wanted, Pam? For me to take it away?'

Pam sighed and looked down at the tear stains on her leggings and on the collar of her 3x-sized purple shirt. 'Yes, Doctor Fefferman. I suppose I did.'

9
THE HERMIT

MAGIC HOUR

'LL TELL YOU what I think about.

The park. Just as the sky turns a bit orange and pink with shots of purple along the tree line. Magic Hour, they call it. Dusk, some say. I miss the wind. Sun. The sound of my shoes on the pavement. I've been told by my new doctor to start at the beginning, so here we are. It was about the moment I'd felt the knife dig into my side for the third time that I knew I was never leaving that house again. And no one was coming in.

The day had started like any other. A list of bullshit punctuated by meals and bathroom breaks. I had taken a long walk in the park near my home. Deadlines were looming and I had to clear my head from the voice of David Reems, Head of Acquisitions, murmuring, 'I sure hope we can make this Anderson account work.' Which I knew was code for 'this better get done.' And I knew exactly what needed to be done: quitting. I had been contemplating it for weeks and tomorrow was the day it was all going to go down. I had written my resignation letter, had been slowly taking personal effects home, copied the contacts of all my clients, and had landed a job with a competitor at a 14% raise.

It was just about having the guts. I'd written my resignation two weeks and six days ago. I was never good at quitting anything. I always let things fall by the wayside and hoped the other party would collapse and take the reins. In dating, with my family, and now with work. I was planning to screw this Anderson issue up so bad they'd have to do the leaving.

I came back through the side gate and locked it behind me, I fully remember that. I waved at Mrs. Barton over the fence even though her dog had dug a hole under it and was determined to only shit in my yard. I came up the back steps and watered the two brown plants on the deck like they stood a chance. I locked the door behind me, all three locks. Safe neighborhood, but if it was worth doing it was worth overdoing, in my opinion. I had a small glass of water by the back window and pricked my finger around the tear in the screen. A small wound bloomed on my fingertip from the sharp thread in the mesh and I jerked back, sucking my finger.

I don't know how long I sat and stared at that wound in the screen. Wondering what I'd do about it tomorrow amid Davis freaking out and stopping by Parson's for a bottle of well-deserved Sauvignon.

A sharp wind blew behind me, then a blow to my head sent everything to black. I fussed in confusion and the discomfort of a heaviness on my chest. I struggled to breathe. I opened my eyes to meet the stare of the solid, heavy eyes of a man in black sitting on my chest. His fingers coiled around my neck, squeezing. I remember flailing and catching my hand on the milk glass vase and crashing it into his forehead. He stumbled back in a daze, and I pushed him off and tumbled out of my dining room and screamed. He caught my foot, sending my face to the floor. I rolled over in a stupor and felt the first sharp slice into my side. I gasped hard, sending the blood from my broken nose into my mouth. Another slice. He turned the knife on the way out this time, causing me to scream once more, before he clasped a hand that stank of gas and metal over my mouth. Another slice to my right hand from wrist to base of my ring finger. One last thrust of the knife and he glazed over. The world became hazy and warm. Like falling asleep in the sun. I blinked to blackness again as I heard the water rush on. I heard my name softly and then it was over.

Mrs. Barton heard the commotion and called the police.

Four days I spent in the hospital. Thank God for busy bodies.

He missed my right lung by an inch, and my life was spared. Stitched up and homebound, it was the first time I saw the aftermath, the precursor, the whole sordid ruckus. The back steps. The crushed plants. The tear in the screen in my kitchen window pulled wide enough to fit through was now bloody. The sink faucet crushed, sending water volcanizing out. The water. My brother had hammered a large piece of plywood to the window until we could 'get it fixed.' But I didn't want it fixed. It sung to me. I wanted more. The palettes came the next day, and I worked to board every window in the house, blocking out any new human hurricane wishing to annihilate me again. I laughed for the first time.

Safe at last.

Next came the blood. The blood. I hadn't had the heart to wash it off, to forget, so there it sat for weeks, then a month. Sometimes I laid on top. Messages from David, the Head of Acquisitions, piled up. First concern; then actionable, yet tempered, teeth-gritted concern. He would have to do the leaving.

I loved being alone, and yet I was inconsolable by the nighttime. I developed palpitations at the slightest sound. I couldn't use a knife properly. I'd been asked to join a support group, but I declined. Too much advice starting with 'Many people'. Many people experience the fear of another break-in. Many people struggle with panic attacks. Many people feel uncomfortable, have heightened alertness, and experience agoraphobia. Many people become obsessive about home safety. I wouldn't say I was obsessive. I'd only boarded my windows up. And fitted my doors with a five-deadbolt system. I'd installed cameras all through the house. I'd pulled up noisy floorboards to decrease the creaking that sends off my nerves. I'd taken all the heavy blankets and put them in the basement, so the weight wasn't on me when I finally fell asleep for those few hours before I was up by dawn to watch the small bit of purple and orange come through a small knot in the plywood high atop the bedroom window. I carved my social security number into my leg so that if I was found outside of the home, I would not be a Jane Doe. A man spoke to me at the grocery store the very first time I decided to leave the sanctity of home, and he sounded quite nice, but when I turned, I swore I looked into the eyes of my attacker. I left my trolley where it stood and drove home. I decided to have my groceries delivered to Mrs. Barton from now on. I turned off all the cameras in the home as I had researched that not all closed-circuit television is private. And my skin pricked and rose at the fact that millions of eyes could be on me right now. I pulled up more floorboards as more creaking appeared, so it was sort of a hopscotch through the house as of late. More calls from my brother. The calls from David had stopped.

I'd started turning on all four televisions at night, each at different volumes, to create a constant hum of background chatter, something to mask the creaks, to convince myself, or any possible attacker, that the house wasn't empty. That worked for about a week. Then, one night, the woman on the kitchen TV stopped mid-sentence, turned, and smirked directly at me. I yanked the plug out of the wall, hard enough to rattle the socket, but it didn't matter.

The characters on the living room screen, frozen in their sitcom poses, had already begun following me with their eyes. Slowly, they got up from their chairs and moved closer to the screen, inch by inch, as if they knew something just might happen.

I stumbled upstairs, half hoping it would just be the lull of a midnight soap opera, but a woman from a commercial called out to me. "Come upstairs, Emma," she said softly, my name sliding off her lips like an invitation. "We'll take care of you. All of us."

And with that, I collapsed on the landing.

I fell asleep quite hard and awoke with my hands around my own neck, squeezing. I placed my hand in a bucket of ice for over an hour to numb it, then rolled up a sock and shoved it to the back of my mouth and proceeded to cut all the fingers off my left hand. Surprisingly it was much easier than I thought.

I sat on the edge of the bed last week with a hot tea and watched the purple and orange sky peek through the knothole and I closed my eyes and dreamed of walking in the park. Of loading my food into the trunk. Even of Mrs. Barton's dog.

And then I smelled it. Metal and grease. I snuck into the den, grabbed the hammer, and stepped back into my bedroom. And waited and waited. And then I realized that there was something about that hyacinth and amber glow that soothed me and at the same time terrified me as the precursor to the worst night of my life. It opened the door to all that I once was and left this.

I took the hammer to my eyes that night. Never again did I want to see that Sedona broadcast its false promises to me through the inch of freedom that sat high on my bedroom window. But I'm here now, in this safe place, I presume. No more creaky floorboards, no blood stains, or cameras. No constant small screen conversations around the house. Just the silence and the surprise of what food I'm given and two legs, one arm, and the safety and security of never seeing the Magic Hour again.

I'm sorry, where were we? Oh yes, I'll tell you what I think about.

The park.

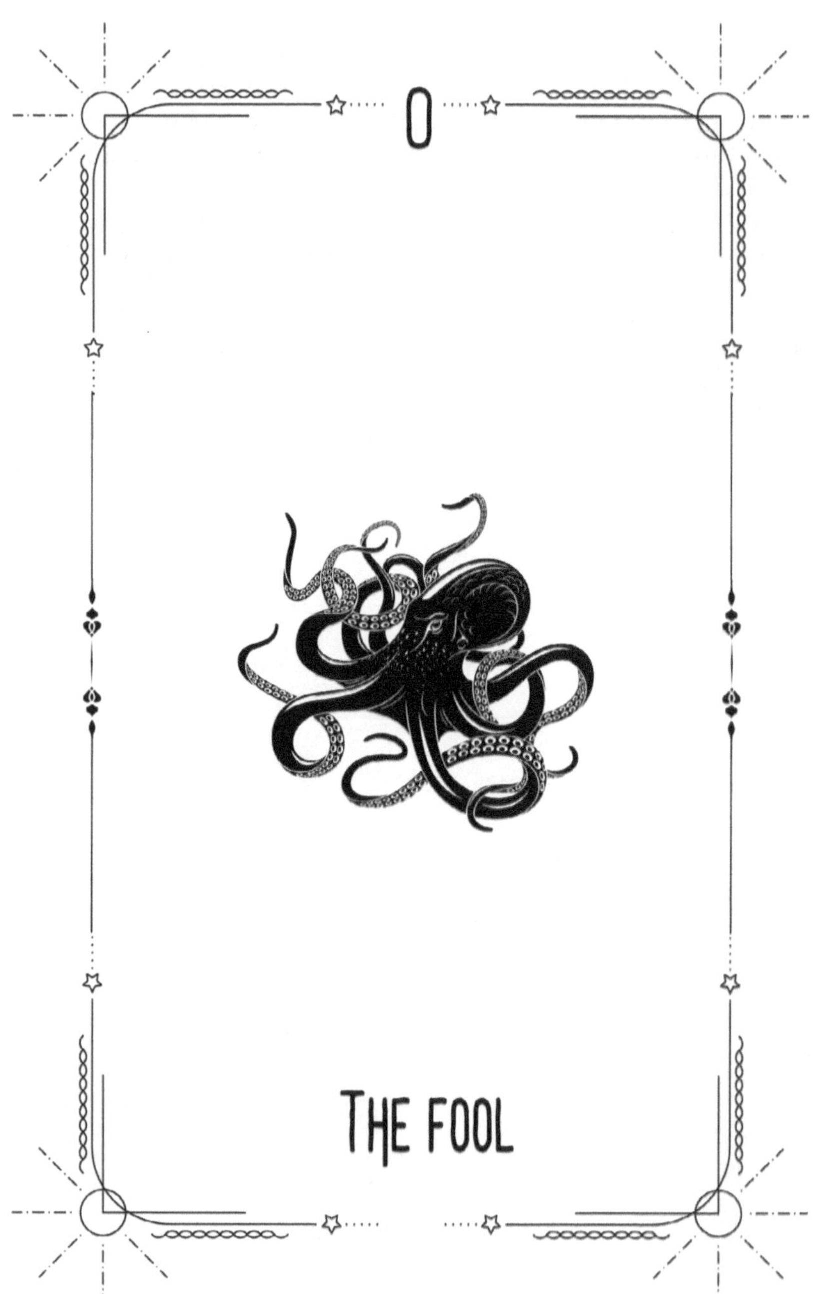

0

THE FOOL

SURFACE

GARRIS EDWARDS AND Charles Vandermen, war-torn and weather-beaten sailors, were petrified, yet ready. From the helm of the dinghy, Charles whispered loudly.

'It's too still out here. You see anything?'

Garris puffed out his chest, his voice betraying him with a slight quiver. 'Just mist.'

Charles' teeth chattered, and he pulled his arms tighter around his chest. 'It's just got everyone spooked, man,' Charles said. 'It's nothing. A sea lion bit Holmes is all. His own fault for jumpin' in.' He looked up to Garris fearfully. 'Right?'.

'Sea lions ain't this close. They ain't got a million teeth like razors, neither.' Garris patted at an ash on his jacket.

'Shut it!' Charles shook. 'You looked in one's mouth?' He spat. 'That thing don't like light neither I heard. Put that camera away!'

The stillness became disturbed by small ripples in the water circling the dinghy.

Garris guffawed. 'I thought you said it was a sea lion. What do they care?'

'Maybe. What're you planning to do with it once you see it?'

'End it.' Garris chewed his cigar and caressed the butt of the stowed gun in his waistband. 'We can't have it killin'. Least of all hangin' about.'

Charles swatted at Garris. 'Put that thing away!'

Garris pointed his camera close to Charles' chin, brushing against his beard hair.

'Or what?'

Charles' eyes widened with terror. He snaked back, scrambling towards the stern. A cavernous mouthful of razor-sharp teeth, at least five feet wide, encircled the port. Garris noticed the shadow out of the corner of his eye. He half turned, flashing the camera, and was bitten swiftly in half. Charles wheezed as Garris' legs fell slowly to the side. He screamed and slapped at his bloodstained face. Garris' blood had trickled into his gaping mouth. The shadow loomed large in front of him as his blue trousers darkened at the crotch.

'I won't. I won't tell a soul, I promise.' Charles whimpered; his hands unconsciously clasped in prayer. Black eyes flashed, blinking multiple sets of eyelids, kaleidoscoping Charles' shivering body.

The teeth enveloped the boat. And the water was still once again.

My steward McCarthy has told me that story half a dozen times, and I only believed he was half right. But I'll tell you now, clear as day, that he couldn't have been more correct. You may say I'm just building a tall tale, the old sailor's way, but had I not seen it, felt it, why I'd think the same. The words of a changed man carry two different weights. On one hand, tall fables of war, fight, or struggle, make the listener's ears grow keener, their mouths hold space for the disbelief to hang there.

On the other, tales of otherworldly stories of the uncanny and the unbelievable find the listener's body taken aback, poised to the right, hands folded as if to say, 'Hmmm, let's see if I buy what he's sellin'.'

And I see you, perched to the right, head cocked, chin pointed at me. That's fine. But you wouldn't be here in the corner of this little tavern if you didn't want to buy a little something, so here we go.

Days on the dock were getting aggressively colder, and the daylight, shorter. And there's always something moving in the water, I've seen it. At first, I couldn't wait to tell any of the men. Now I kept it to myself to avoid the whispers of my impending insanity.

Every day, dozens of men scrambled on the dock, rotating within their jobs, shouting orders. We were all dirty and exhausted, looking alike in our newsboy caps, dungarees, and heavy raincoats. One day, a kid by the name of Fritz, the same age as me, died. Our fourth death on the docks in two months. Got hit by a pallet, knocking him into the water. Took 'em forever to find him. After a while, they gave up and just let his stiff body float to the surface. Simply, he drowned. Well, that's what they said, but there was no accounting for all the bite marks on his legs and slash on his chest.

I saw it again that night. Monster, man, mermaid, I'm not sure. But it was staring this time. My stomach flipped 'cause I knew it caught me staring too.

I was on dawn duty the following day, so I finished my work, headed to the lean-to chow hall, and took a rest in my cot for my 3 AM call time. It was pretty somber that night in the barracks. Something hung heavy in the air, deep enough to feel it in your lungs. Lots of murmurs about Fritz. From the tallest to the smallest tales about what might be in that water. The water we got to haul things into, the water we straddled, trying to lift cargo onto docks.

'What's keeping it from running aground?' was the circulating question.

'A manatee or a small shark, of course. It's got to be, right?' I heard someone say.

It was cold that next morning, so I stole smokes from McCarthy and his bottle of brown liquor to stay warm on watch. He'd been out for days with the drink. Maybe he was dead. I don't know.

I took a swig of McCarthy's bottle after I fully wiped down the top. Who the hell knows what he had? I grabbed the box of smokes upside down and they trickled onto the wet deck like netted fish. I lit a match and scrambled to grab them before they were completely useless and that's when I turned, shocked through by fear. Smooth black eyes staring at me. I grabbed the smokes off the deck and shoved them in my pocket quickly, not givin' a damn if some of them broke. I moved the matchlight to the eyes.

My brain drifted to a place a long time ago. My mother had died in December of '42. I'd never seen my father wince in pain, let alone cry, red-faced like a baby, before that day and the forty-seven days that followed. My brother and I had taken to spending more time outside, so as to leave him be. We'd play and shiver 'til we couldn't stand it, then come in too exhausted to make a rumpus. One day, my father joined us. Warily and quietly, we placed a weak and small snowman together. My father stood watching, grimacing. At once, the small of my back smarted, cold, and wet. I turned to see my father's lips curl, widen to baring teeth to a full-out cackle. A snowball hit my brother square in the shoulder. One after another, they came, my father laughing all the while. The air swelled in misted curls from his mouth. Clouds of hope. I'd never seen him cry since.

Against the navy sky blanketing the dock, my breath left my body in a mass of that same mist and smoke, though absent of hope. My feet were cemented in fear. The eyes stayed. Stayed on me and were closer now. I blinked several times before it all went black, and my head hit the dock.

Seaweed and salt, with a mix of something I still can't place, choked me awake. I opened my eyes and turned over, my hand slipping against the smooth wet rocks. A tight and primitive makeshift cave surrounded me.

How far was I from the dock?

The water was as far as you could see from the dock's edge, no land around.

The eyes came back again, inches from me. I pulled back hard, my wrist skidding against the wet rock as I tried to scream. A slippery, long-fingered hand raised to my mouth. Her skin was the heavenly blue of a cloudless day, her eyes, black, and her hair, flame red.

'Hush,' she said.

She pressed her wet hands to my head and a din so painful took over me. Warming, twisting, and vibrating my insides. The history of all her kind tore through my mind like buzz saw. Our disturbance of her home, our presence in the water, the thickening of the ice, the snow.

But it was the photographs. Every man just like me who swore he saw it, got close enough to capture it, in mind or on film, took a life. The flash of the camera warped their eyes, shrinking them into their sockets and starting a chain reaction of explosions in their brains. And one by one, they all die.

The sights grew more and more gruesome; a sickening loop paced heavily behind my tired eyes. Over and over. A weak apology left my lips as the vibrations took over my face, paralyzing my speech and pinching my throat from the inside out. I came in and out of consciousness, focusing on her eyes and the warmth of her breath. My stomach twisted in pain, and I finally dropped her gaze and realized that I was impaled on a thick blue tentacle that pierced clean through and twisted inside me. Its strange ridges bounced and pulsed along it's bioluminescent veins with each heavy stroke. It curved my spine in on itself and shook it back and forth, and I let out the first painful and blood-filled scream since I landed in that cave.

She pulled my head closer to hers, the sweat of her brow falling gently across my nose and mouth like a spring mist. She hummed and clicked, throwing her head back for moments at a time. The visions of death and destruction faded into moving clouds of light. I couldn't make out if she was enrobed in such a light, or if the power behind my eyes created a permanent haze. I caught myself looking from her pulsing tentacle to her exposed neck and mouth now agape. I winced and grab onto her neck in a forceful grasp, clinging to her as the pain suddenly ruptured into extreme pleasure. My body shook with a never before felt rhythm as her clicks grew louder into chirps. I moaned loudly, softening my grip on her gorgeous blue neck and pulling my fingers through her bright hair. I couldn't help but pull, my body was not my own and I knew that any moment I would explode.

The echoes of the hollow cave only magnified the wet and guttural sounds that escaped us. The air, already heavy with sea mist, caught us entangled in a saccharine twist. I pulled her closer to me, her massive body looming over, and leaned gently. Completely possessed, I licked at her neck like a madman. Her sweat was like honey. A redness took over the cave as her tentacle twitched faster, sending me to my limit. I expelled, embarrassed. And I stared at fourteen versions of my expression of complete satisfaction through her mirrored eyes. She let go slowly as her breath still danced around me. The tentacle flipped flaccidly out of me, and I dropped, the stone floor coming quickly.

A daylight streak of weak winter sunshine woke me.

She stood over me, three times my size. Her features had grown rigid, more angular, like a tall Grecian sculpture. She was quite beautiful, and I found myself staring, wanting her again.

'It won't be long now. Rest.' She went to close my eyes with one of her long fingers and I caught her hand softly.

'Why am I here?' I croaked out, still hoarse from my earlier exclamations.

'We are dying, we must endure.' Her voice was a gargle. 'We have wasted too much time.'

She rubbed my bare stomach with her free hand because I wouldn't let go. I looked down, and the shock sent me reeling away from her. I tried to scream with all my might, and nothing came but a dry holler.

'Don't move! You're delicate!' She shouted, her eyes fearful.

My stomach was distended and full of something that swam and stretched inside of me. There were many, or just a few, I'm not sure. She inched forward to cradle my head and then slid her long hand down to place it over my mouth.

'It is time. Bite!' she ordered.

I bit down and she unfurled a long claw from her finger and made a quick slice into my abdomen. My scream was clouded by her hand and the sugar-sweet steam trickled down my throat, stealing the salt-air bitterness from my tongue. A continuous plop echoed in the cave and soft circular sacks spilled out of me by the dozens. She gently unclasped her hand from my teeth, pulled open a flap on her smooth white belly, and began to quickly gather the sacks.

'Thank you. Thank you,' she said, scrambling for the sacks. Her hands flowed with thick liquid and blood.

'Why? Why?' All I could muster was a small whisper. The cave was spinning and falling away from me.

'Because we are dying. You are helping us live. Our children will live.'

I held my hand out. She was further away than I thought, and I mistakenly swatted at her. She clasped my hand in both of hers and looked at me for a long time. I finally took stock of her many sets of eyelids, gills, ridges. My vision was darkened by a mix of blood loss and fear. She reared her head back before I went completely dark and released a large amount of liquid from her mouth. It seared my stomach, and with that, I was out again.

I woke up on the edge of the dock, body stiff. All at once, I was conscious of my recent surgery, and I yanked my heavy coat off and lifted my shirt. A light burn, the size of my fist. That was it. That was all.

SURFACE

I raised myself on my elbows and saw her, fifty yards away, joined by twenty other sets of small black eyes. I didn't know what to do but nod. That was all I could offer. To her, to my children.

I licked my lips and basked in the last of the sweetness of her. For she was no man, no mermaid, no monster, but will forever be my mistress.

Do with that story what you will and enjoy the last of your whiskey. I can't stomach the bitter taste of it after that morning. I prefer sweet these days.

2
HIGH PRIESTESS

THE SEVERITY OF THINGS

MITCH SCRATCHED AT the scab behind his ear. The end of his glasses arm had broken off. A small casualty. He'd taken to wrapping it in poster gum, waiting to gather enough savings for the next pair of glasses. It'd do 'til then.

He'd grown an odd fondness for feeling the bump that gathered beneath the scab. It became a nervous tick, then an unwinding mechanism, and eventually a habit. He'd been saving for glasses going on six months, now. But Christa's engagement ring came first.

At the end of their third year together, Mitch had rented a snowy cabin in the Adirondacks. Small by all trappings, but it had her list of wants fully squared away: a hot tub, a fireplace, a cozy bed, a woodland view, and for some reason, lots of antlers. It was there that Mitch bent the knee, Christa yelped, then cried, and all was right with the world.

Today, Mitch stood stooped over a row of wheelchairs, three years older, with a Gerontology degree from Stonybrook and a steady job as a public health advocate. Still stuck in the 40K plus bracket and still paying off Christa's ring. They'd downsized at EverGreen Care and shifts became a bit heavier for the senior staff. Mitch was lucky when he worked less than fifty-five hours a week.

Salary. A few months more of this and he and Christa could be expecting an eviction notice. Mr. Calaree, the landlord at the Windy Meadow Townhomes (another one of Christa's wants: a three-floor townhome in the woods) was kind enough to wait one to three days after rent was due. Today, they were staring down the barrel of thirteen days. Walking into the rental office, his head low, Mitch noticed Mr. Calaree's empty desk. Hurriedly, he slapped the envelope on it and walked out. The jingle bells attached to the front door mingled with a muffled, 'Hello?.'

Mitch walked hard along the parking lot and didn't look back.

This Thursday afternoon hit him square in the face with the soft smell of oncoming death and the turkey gravy that would pepper today's lunch special at EverGreen Care. The first scent was something he couldn't speak to anyone about. Not anyone outside the healthcare industry at any rate.

'I have a very hard time believing you can smell death, Mitch. That's so morbid. Why would you say that?' Christa had told him once over dinner.

'Because you can. Ask any nurse or doctor who works in geriatrics. There's a certain whiff on the air. Not putrid, just sweet, heavy. It's unmistakable.'

Christa pushed her meat around her plate, irritated. 'Just awful, and so nonchalant. Those poor people. I hope you don't tell them these things.'

Mitch stared indignantly as Christa slowly lifted her gaze to him.

'Of course not, honey, that would be terrible.'

'Indeed.'

They would finish their dinner in silence.

Heading into the Edelweiss C Wing of EverGreen Care, Mitch skirted around a large family gathered in one room, spilling into the hallway. All sobs and head shakes. The man in the hospital bed sat gleefully, shaking the hands of those around him. His lips slightly parted in joy; the ends curled into a modest smile. They held no color, seeming to melt into the rest of his face. He lay back gently, and everyone pounced forward and eventually leaned back as

the man's mouth relaxed into what looked like the beginnings of an early morning yawn. A wail cut through the crowd. A diminutive woman was being propped up by two men, red-faced and somber. Mitch stared deeply at the man in the bed.

His mouth hung wider, lower, wider still. A loud crack shot through the woman's wailing and the man's jaw slacked a good five inches, landing on the shoulder of his mandala-patterned hospital gown. Mitch's breath shallowed as the gaping hole stared back at him. He pressed his hand hard on the glass, turning everyone's attention to him. People in the dead man's room came spilling out. Looks of bewilderment streaked with disdain. A man pushed past two women in the doorway.

'This is a private moment! Do you mind?'

Mitch gasped for air. 'I'm sorry, that's . . . that's my patient this afternoon. I'm just stunned.'

It was the only lie he could think of. He couldn't remember seeing this man on this floor even once before. Maybe the pallid condition of his skin confused him, maybe he'd been there for ages.

The man's eyes softened. A woman in a large brown coat came up behind him.

'I'm so sorry, sir. We're all very sad. Long time coming. Come on, Jim.' The woman pulled the man along back to the room.

The wailing woman was now seated, and folks began to trickle out of the room. Some nodded to Mitch sheepishly, some ignoring him completely. Mitch focused on the man's mouth. The same early morning yawn that let out his final breath.

A small tap on his shoulder pulled him achingly out of his trance. He jumped.

'Oof! Touchy! You okay?' A red-headed woman in bright pink scrubs rubbed Mitch's back lightly. Olivia, ever the space invader.

He stepped back instinctively, giving the approaching EverGreen 'Recovery' Team more headway to get into the room with the deceased. 'Yeah, just.' Mitch pointed.

'Mmmhmm. A day in the life. Or not. Come on, Debra wants to see you.'

EverGreen Care, part of the larger Windsong Inc., was a sprawling adult care complex with three 'steps,' as they called them. The first 'step' was Autumn Sky Adult Village, for the still-active seniors with community events, singles dances, and the ever-present Pinochle game. Next came Moonlight Mist Retirement Center, for those aging out of wanting to attend a community event, those attached to an apparatus or those simply throwing in the towel of wanting to live alone. At Moonlight Mist, everyone had a roommate, which was ninety percent good. The aching ten percent was a stew of cantankerous attitudes mixed with practical jokes and the weakest punches ever thrown. Few and far between, though. Mitch ran between Moonlight Mist and the final 'step,' Edelweiss, the end-of-life care facility. It was referred to as

'Gentle Hospice,' as the employee packet from Windsong Inc. stated. Mitch remembered giggling to himself in the onboard meeting room while reading the text. A few senior members had stared and raised eyebrows, including the COO of Windsong, Mary Connely. Mary Connely had spent two decades working for Marriott until downsizing in 2005 sent her packing to Tampax. In 2007 she ended up acquiring Windsong Inc., a low-budget adult complex that she turned into more of an adult resort. Mitch hadn't seen her meet one resident; she actually seemed to fear the elderly. Death was inevitable, so she picked a great racket to pursue.

'Mitch, was there something you'd like to share?' Mary Connely asked him coldly.

'Well, yes. 'Gentle Hospice' is a bit silly, isn't it? Who wants 'heavy' or 'forced' hospice? Just a thought to revise the text.'

He stared forward, unashamed of his statement.

I'm literally the most qualified one in the room, you fucks, and gentle hospice sounds stupid.' He thought.

'I'm so sorry, continue, Mary.'

Mary's eyes widened, she cleared her throat and continued. The 2009 revision removed 'Gentle Hospice' and replaced it with 'Compassionate Care.'

'Helllooooo." Olivia's toothy smile broke him out of his stupor. 'You're not in trouble, you know,' Olivia said.

'Hmm?' Mitch was still thinking of the man in the bed.

'With Debra. You're not in trouble. Actually, I think it's a favor she needs from you.'

'That's never good.' Mitch thought back on his last three years with EverGreen Care. It was a tough job. All the loss, the grieving, the clock ticking, for all of them. It was getting attached to people and having to let go. Keeping secrets they wouldn't dare tell their families, keeping secrets he should definitely go to the authorities about. But mostly, it was in that bittersweetness that he found his calling: reminding people of their worth. Most forget what they've meant to others as they lay dying.

As they rounded the corner, Debra, a tall woman in a grey suit—only ever a grey suit—was already outside of her office.

'I'll leave you to it.' Olivia tapped Mitch on the shoulder and briskly scattered away.

'Where are you going?' Mitch looked lost.

'It's Turkey and Gravy Day!' Olivia turned back on her heel and skirted away.

Mitch turned back to Debra, whose face was graced with a tight grin that met everything but her eyes.

'You wanted to see me?'

'Yes, Mitch, please, come sit.' Debra closed the door tightly behind them. She stood for a moment behind her equally tall desk and sat slowly. Clasping her hands tightly together, she began.

'As you know, EverGreen has seen a few cuts in the last two years.'

'Oh no.' Mitch couldn't help but groan.

'Oh no! Mitch we're not letting you go for anything!'

His back relaxed.

'I have a proposition for you. We're struggling to fulfill an arm of Windsong, Operation Icebox.'

'The Meals on Wheels thing?' Mitch sat back, feeling a hell of a lot better knowing he wouldn't have to explain to Christa that he lost his job in what she already called 'a creepy and dead-end industry.' The only proof she'd needed to get him to work for her dad's insurance company.

'Yes, we've lost a few route takers due to college, and they need someone on the Jackson route. Now there's only six stops there and we don't dare abandon the route, but it's not the best of all neighborhoods so we can't retain anyone.'

'Ha, you don't know where I grew up.'

'The reason why I wanted to talk to you is that I'd like this to, hmm...' She paused. 'I'd like you to take on the role of director for the program in this area.'

'Wow, um, thank you, this is really nice, but I'm already here like fifty hours a week.' Mitch sighed.

'Oh, see I've got an idea for that. What I'm going to do is give you one-half day here, we've just hired a part-timer, so you can dedicate some time to the route. You'll only need about three hours for the Icebox run, I'll just not, eh, tell them. Oh! And as a director that comes with an additional twenty-three thousand a year. Effective immediately.'

'Are you fucking serious?' Mitch stared incredulously. 'I mean, why are you doing this?'

'Because you have no idea how hard it is to find people that care. Really care about these people. Not the Harry and Mary Connely's of the world. The people here at the grassroots, making meager earnings. Mitch, someday you're gonna take over for me. You've earned a thank you, in the only way that matters. In money. Those two roles should put you over sixty-eight a year.'

'Deb, this is awesome, I can't thank you enough. What can I do to repay you?'

'Just please give me another three to five years.'

'Done. What day do I take over the route?'

'Tomorrow.'

Mitch bristled. Christa's birthday.

Mitch bounded up the five steps of 14 Birch Way with a spring in his heel he hadn't felt since the morning after he asked Christa to marry him. Things were going to change and change quickly. No more dodging Mr. Calaree, no more buying Top Ramen 20-packs towards the end of the month, no more stealing toilet paper from work. He could fund the life Christa wanted. Her beautiful townhome view of the woods. In winter, he loved watching her drink her coffee leaning on the dining room window, quietly gasping at the slew of deer that would gather in the backyards. Maybe they could even revisit the talk of children. The door was already open as he darted in.

'Babe? Christa? Where are you?'

A small whimper came from the dining room, followed by mumbling. Mitch's heart sank hoping he hadn't caught her with someone.

'Babe?' He moved through the home to the dining room.

There sat Christa at the head of the table, her usual station, the deer-watching seat. Standing next to her was Erin, Christa's younger sister, with a smug grin. Erin Marksley was four years younger than Christa and much more successful. Erin had been the good girl and joined Daddy's insurance firm straight out of high school. She was even their spokesperson in local commercials before Bernard Marksley purchased Lincoln Securities, a very stable and cash-rich commodity after the owner died and the sons, heavy into another cash cow, scrap metal, didn't want to have anything to do with it. Within three years, the Marksley portfolio grew fifteen-fold, making Erin a high six-figure earner by the time she was twenty-two. Now twenty-five, she stood in Christa and

Mitch's modest townhome, digging her stiletto heels into their low-middle-class linoleum.

'Oh, hey Erin.' He paused, looking from Christa to Erin and back. 'Everything alright?'

'No Mitch,' Christa sniffed, 'It's not. Erin, I'd like some time alone with Mitch.'

'Of course.' Erin nodded, never taking her eyes off Mitch. 'I've got some calls to make anyway.' Erin clicked her way into the foyer.

'Christa, what's going on?' Mitch sat slowly, instinctively grasping for her hand which she curtly pulled away.

'Mitch, I'm tired. I'm tired of living this way. Paycheck to paycheck, no social life, no social standing. I haven't bought a new article of clothing for myself in two years. Two years, Mitch! We're scrimping and saving and then the savings go and you're refusing to leave a job that drains you, drains us. Drains our bank accounts.'

'My job doesn't drain our bank accounts.' Mitch's spine straightened.

'Oh yes, I forgot, it doesn't put anything in there to begin with.'

'And your part-time shift at Marshall's does?'

Christa sat back sharply.

'Fuck you, Mitch! This is insane!'

'What's insane is that you're always making me the bad guy. I make us poor. Me! Meanwhile, you got the two-carat rock you wanted, I co-signed for the Jeep you wanted, and I found this townhouse you begged me to pay twenty-eight hundred a month for because 'if we split it, we can totally make it work.' That lasted all of four months when you said you were struggling and stopped paying the rent altogether. But yes, I'm the problem. None of this matters anyway because there's gonna be some big changes.'

The clicks returned. 'You're damn right there are. Christa, just get to the point.' Erin perused her meticulous manicure, bored.

Mitch stood quickly, knocking back the chair without retort. 'What does she mean? Christa?!'

Christa slowly pulled the pear-shaped diamond off her left hand and placed it quietly on the table. Erin joined her sister at the head of the table, cradling both of her shoulders in her hands.

'Tell him.'

'Mitch. It's over. I can't do this anymore. We want different things. You want to take it slow. And I want to stop having to explain to my family that we've not yet set a date. We're nowhere near starting a family. You embarrass me and you don't care. Erin's going to be taking me on as her secretary. I'll be clearing more than you make in a year by myself. And I'll be keeping the townhouse.'

Mitch reached behind him and slowly lifted the chair, placing it squarely in its place.

'Is this what you really want?'

Erin chirped, 'Yes, it's what she really wants.'

'I was asking Christa.' Mitch's eyes softened and began to redden. 'Is it?'

Christa nodded and looked at her lap.

'Well, then. I'll be expecting your things out by tomorrow.'

A chorus of expletive-laden shouts enveloped the dining room. 'Are you fucking serious? This is my dream home.'

'But you aren't on the lease. And you haven't been paying for it.'

'Fuck you, I'm not on the lease. I signed it!'

'I signed first, then added you when we moved in, and when you stopped paying, I...' Mitch crossed his arms and leaned against the wall abutting the kitchen. 'I got angry and took you off. I'd all but forgotten until now.'

'Why would you do that?' Christa whispered and stood slowly from the chair. Erin crossed her arms tightly and narrowed her eyes to Mitch who gazed lazily in her direction and then back to Christa.

'To protect myself, I guess. Everything I've done has been for you. The trips, the townhome, the job for the 401K and the pension, the debt. All for you, because I loved you. I *love* you. Even as you stand here and leave me, I love you. But I agree with you. We want different things. I want you to want to love me. And I—.' Mitch sighed heavily and wiped his eyes. 'I don't know what you want, and I'm sorry for that. But I would like you to find another life that doesn't constantly disrupt mine. That doesn't constantly demean my life's work or my hopes. I want you as far away from this place as possible.'

'My sister is going to have to completely start from scratch, how could you be so fucking cruel?!'

'Oh Erin, don't act like she doesn't want just that.' As he moved toward the dining table, Christa stood defiantly, and Erin stepped in between the two of them.

'Here is the chance you've been waiting for to re-invent yourself, Christa. No longer living like a pauper to your family of princes. I truly wish you all the happiness in the world.'

Christa began to sob. 'I'm coming back tomorrow and I'm taking everything!'

'Please do. They're all your design choices anyway.'

Erin chuckled as she tried to restrain a wailing Christa.

'What're you gonna sleep on? A mattress you got from the old folk's home?'

'No. I'm going to refurnish it.'

Christa pushed through Erin's grasp. 'With what? Someone leave you an inheritance?!'

'Oh, Christa. I was coming home to tell you I'd just gotten a twenty-thousand-dollar raise. Effective immediately. Isn't that wonderful?'

Christa stepped back on her heel. 'What? You did?' Christa turned to Erin, who desperately searched for something in the home to look at other than her ailing sister.

'It's a thank you for being so dedicated to my work. I'm really excited about it.'

'We could afford this place for once.' Christa's face softened and gradually found the bits and pieces of regret. Her brow furrowed and tightened. She looked longingly around the home, settling on the view of the wooden horizon out the dining room window.

'I'm sorry, Mitch. I-I should have listened. I should've let you tell me. I'm very proud of you.' She leaned into him, and he held her tightly. Erin rolled her eyes and checked her watch.

'It's alright. You'd made your decision anyway. I do wish you the best of everything.'

'I was just angry, I—' Christa began to shake her head violently and a sharp gasp left her. Her gaze settled on the window as three deer sprinted along the tree line and then disappeared out of sight.

Erin came up behind her and pulled her away from Mitch. Christa clung tightly at first and loosened her grip, defeated.

'Come on, Christa, let's go.'

Something in Erin's voice sounded like bad advice given. As if she'd expected Mitch to have a poor hand.

'I'll make sure my things are out by tomorrow,' Christa said weakly without turning around. Mitch made no move. He didn't even turn to see her leave. The front door clicked and let out its tension-friendly steeliness, shutting Christa out of his life forever.

Mitch stood for a moment and lost himself in the awkward lightness he felt for a flash of time. He wandered over to the dining room window. The deer were gone, and the sun began to set, blanketing the field in a pink and purple haze. A singular cloud sat in the sky, separating them into two as the earth turned them apart. A fine hole stretched into an oval, longer still against the cotton candy sky. The beginnings of a morning yawn. Mitch's eyes widened. He quickly closed the blinds.

The Friday morning commute to the headquarters of Operation Icebox found the world a little too still for Mitch's taste. He'd woken up alone, as expected, and the house was quiet, as expected, but something lingered in the air that morning that he couldn't put his finger on. It wasn't the death smell. No, it was a heaviness, a harbinger. He'd wondered if he'd jumped the gun at Debra's proposal. The paperwork for the role was already in his inbox when he woke, Debra made sure of that. But having three hours to hit only six homes with meals seemed like a vacation. He should be happy, ecstatic even, but the pang of Christa sat in his stomach like a boulder. He'd jumped at the chance to provide more for her. He felt harsh for not fighting for it. For not giving in and being accountable for being a near-destitute jackass. The groveling was what she wanted, it had gotten worse, and admitting defeat was something he'd grow accustomed to. Throwing his hands up, throwing in the towel. He'd thought about how useless she'd make him feel. How many other degrees he could have gotten, how joining the family biz on merit could've put them on easy street.

Would life be harder or easier without her in it? The minute he stepped foot out of his car and grabbed the keys to one of the project vans, he was making his choice. He was moving on. He'd sit for another fifteen minutes. Time felt like a construct now, mostly because he'd also left home an hour earlier than he needed to.

The futile act of trying to put his keys in his pocket was anxiety-inducing. They'd been a menace since Christa twined a glass-breaking device onto his keychain, after she'd locked the keys in the Jeep on one of their woodland jaunts. He'd tried in vain to get it off, but even with bolt cutters it wouldn't budge. A giant purple icicle hung from a single house key, car key and a set of EverGreen keys with a pine tree emblem. He crunched along the parking lot, peeks of autumn frost gathering beneath his canvas sneakers. He walked through an open orange steel door that looked like it belonged in a chop shop and was greeted by an older Black gentleman.

'You must be Mitch Monahan. Debra said you'd be here with bells on. I've been listening for 'em.' The man chuckled to himself. 'Otis P. Adams. Route Coordinator.'

Otis extended his hand. Mitch quickly grabbed it and shook vigorously. The man's smooth timbre put him at ease.

'Yes! Hi, good morning. So nice to meet you.' Mitch smiled and marked the good feeling pushing the boulder in his stomach aside.

'Come on back into the office, I'll give you a low down on the route.'

'You want me to close this?' Mitch pointed at the orange door.

'Nah, there's a raccoon in here, he'll find his way out.'

Mitch followed Otis briskly.

Their wet shoes squeaked along a linoleum hallway into a windowed office adorned with green metal office furniture. Mitch took the first red chair in front of Otis's desk.

'The Jackson route. Mmm, mmm, mmm.' Otis raised his eyebrows and looked Mitch up and down. A tall, pale lank of a man. Maybe one sixty, on a wet day.

'Yeah, Debra said it was a rough route.'

'Not rough per se, all the residents are kind and safe. It's just the way there that creeps 'em out.'

'Creeps who out?' Mitch leaned into Otis' desk trying to see what was on the route paperwork.

'I'm sure Deb's told you that we haven't been able to retain folks on this route. Something in the air in the neighborhood. Eerie.'

'Jackson isn't that bad. I grew up in Willis, the next town over. Nothing eerie about it. Just drugs. Lots of 'em.'

'I would've never pegged you for Willis.' Otis laughed aloud. 'Amherst yes, but not Willis.' He wheezed and Mitch laughed.

'Yeah well, my mom was on drugs, a lot of them. So, my aunt took me in and raised me in...' he paused, 'Amherst.'

Otis howled. 'I knew it.' A raucous laugh from the two mingled in the office.

'But seriously, is it a ghost town?'

'Nah, nothing like that. Honestly, I think it comes from one resident in particular.' Otis pulled a manilla folder from under his stack of paperwork and plunked it down in front of Mitch.

'Lucy Gilsman, seventy-two. Lives at 13 Hockaborne Way, 10 A.' Mitch opened the folder and lingered on the photo attached. An elderly woman with wild white hair, deep-set brown eyes, and thin lips. The photo behind it was a brunette woman in middle age, with a bright smile. Her white and blue striped tunic blew in the wind.

'Are these the same woman?' Mitch continued to thumb through the paperwork: dietary suggestions, allergies.

'The very same. Lucy began to exhibit strange behavior after the death of her husband, Gustavo, about seven years ago. Hoarding, her bathing became erratic to almost non-existent and became completely reclusive about two years ago.' Otis peered over his desk to look at the folder.

'So, what's her story? Just creepy to the drivers or what?' Mitch focused on the smiling woman in the photo.

His eyes traveled all around the image until it landed on a pale face in the background. It seemed to hover behind her with no clear body being attached to it.

'It's like I said, she's been reclusive. She never opens the door for the meals, we just knock. But every driver says it sounds like there is something in there with

her. Something, I don't know, evil sounding.'

'Really?' Mitch was fixated on the pale face. 'Well, no better time to find out.'

He closed the folder and handed it over to Otis.

'Keep it, and here's the rest of your route. All good people.' Otis stood and grabbed a set of keys hung by a bright yellow ribbon.

'It's van five in the garage; they're all numbered in the windshield. All are stocked for the route in the freezer in the back. Everyone gets a box of meat, a burlap sack of veggies, and a small tote of dairy. You should be able to carry it in one swoop.' Otis handed the keys to Mitch.

'Awesome, thanks! I'm excited to get started. Hey, it was really cool to meet you, Otis, I hope to see more of you.' Mitch grinned at the keys and noticed Otis hadn't let go.

'Just be careful with 10 A. Don't let it get inside your head.'

'Let what get inside?'

Otis pointed in the direction of the garage where the errant raccoon had hopefully escaped from. 'Van five.' Otis grinned as Mitch nodded away.

It would have been a smart choice to get 10 A out of the way and get the fuss over. But saving it for last made Mitch feel better. Anything that happened at that residence might spoil the rest of the route and he wanted to meet these new residents as responsive as he could be.

Melody Jones, 80, 54 Perbauch Street, a one- bedroom, green shutter board home tucked next to a Greek Bakery, couldn't wait to get her delivery. Kind, and loquacious, finished one cigarette and lit up another as Mitch laid the packages inside her front door. She loved the pecan pie as a treat during the Fourth of July week and shared a bit of gossip that Gary Faulkner is cheating on his wife and may have another illegitimate son somewhere. Mitch had no idea if he should know this errant Mr. Faulkner or not, but he nodded just the same.

Matt St. James, 73, 9 Jensen Avenue, Apt B, small talk, watched as Mitch struggled to keep the door open and lay the packages down. Shook his head from side to side like he surely could've been more graceful, patted Mitch on the back, shut the door, and locked it.

George Finney, 75, 40 Olivera Avenue C4 Rear, Mitch scratched the sides of the side mirrors of the van backing up, knocked once, loudly the second time. The door swung open to a large floor-set console television with two VCRs stacked on top. Moans and high-pitched screams echoed into the back lot from some dated porno Mr. Finney was consuming in his short red robe and no pants.

'Well come on if you're coming.' Mr. Finney ushered Mitch in quickly and slammed the door on him upon leaving. Mitch hurried to the van.

Caroline Baum, 81, 19 Fall Street, 4A, quiet, kind, wrung a doily in her hand the whole time. The house was filled with milk glass and figurines. Mitch set the packages down in the middle of the kitchen free from the fragile fray. She gave him one dollar, which he returned quickly.

'On the house, ma'am. Have a good day.'

Emma Coates, 71, 39 Orlean Street 3H, not one word uttered, just nodding, closed the door with a smile on departing.

Mitch stood on the street staring at the low apartment house at 13 Hockaborne Way. Unassuming, prison-grey with navy shutters on the front eight windows. Mitch pulled the final packages from the van freezer and watched as it shut slowly. He turned and screamed, knocking the dairy tote loose. A young boy stood behind him, stern. Mitch scrambled to check the small jugs and plastic tubs of dairy for breakage and looked quizzically at the boy.

'What're you doing?' Mitch asked tight-lipped.

'You going in there?' The boy pointed to the apartment building without looking at it.

'Yes. I have to deliver this food to a needy woman inside. It could've broken.'

'Don't go in there. People go in there and they don't come out. Not all the way.' The boy finally looked at the building.

'You mean they get lost?' Mitch tried to kneel at the boy's level without spilling the goods.

'You better get lost, Mister.' And at that, the boy shot down the street.

Mitch heaved a heavy sigh. 'Fuck me.'

The front doorknob to the building was loose. Quite concerning in a heavy neighborhood such as this, but the graffiti that adorned the walls and doors of apartments 1A through 5A held a reason to feel that the outside world had no intention of coming here.

It will chew on your soul! Don't let it out! She screams; he beams.

Waste her. Don't feed the animal. God won't come here.

'Well, this seems great.'

The busy and gritty street sounds seemed to fade as Mitch walked deeper down the corridor. He passed the stairwell to the second floor, which suggested it had been abandoned long ago. From the third step to the ninth, a large hole sat, collecting dust, debris, and the occasional leaf. The second-floor landing window had broken, letting whatever the world wanted to throw into it enter undisturbed.

6A, 7A, 8A, and 9A's doors had been broken off their hinges and exposed themselves to the hallway. 8A looked like someone stood up from their chair and walked clean out of the apartment. All the furnishings were still lovingly in their place, meager accommodations to say the least. Nothing in the open room matched and it reminded him warmly of his and Christa's first apartment. The graffiti on the adjoining wall knocked him back to the world of 10A.

LET HER BURN IN HELL.

10A stood squarely in front of him. He consciously wiped the pool of drool that crept across the side of his mouth and dabbed at his forehead. Shit. Could he do this every week? His stomach protested the egg sandwich he'd stopped to get before heading to Ms. Jones' on Perbauch. He set the packages down in front of the door and loudly knocked three times. And waited. And waited.

He lifted his fist to knock again and that was when his head grabbed a din from thin air. A crowd full of chattering; voices, teeth, scales, the blended sounds of nails scratching against chalkboards, and metal.

He turned away from the door, head spinning. As the thick clangor subsided, each voice and row leaving the party, one sound rang clear. The wet sound of a throaty whisper. Words unclear; Mitch instinctively put his ear to the door. The whisper grew louder and found its footing in a guttural moan.

Mitch ran swiftly down the hallway grasping the loose front doorknob with a soaked hand.

Click.

Mitch turned shyly to see the door of 10A ajar. A small woman with wild white hair stood deep inside the apartment, several feet away from the door.

'Mrs. Gilsman? M-my name is Mitch; I'll be here every Wednesday. The food is there in front of your door. You take care now.'

Sneaking a quick peek at the woman once more he noticed something familiar: the pale face. Mitch turned his full body towards 10A.

'Mrs. Gilsman?'

The door slammed heavily, knocking dust into his hair, and sending further debris down the gaping hole between steps three and nine.

Mitch walked briskly to the truck, now lined up by four new boys with crossed arms.

'Your shirt's all wet.' The first boy scoffed.

'He told you not to go there, dumbass.' The second peddled away on a spray-painted girl's bike.

Mitch looked down at the deep blue V on his light blue sweatshirt. He couldn't remember getting in the van much less starting the ignition. Mitch was pulling into the Operation Icebox parking lot before he regained any sense of who he was.

A jingly thud echoed into Otis's office. Mitch dropped the keys and folders on his desk.

'I don't think this is going to work out.' Mitch hadn't realized how out of breath he'd become or how dry his mouth was. He took a deep breath, more ragged sounding than he intended.

'Damn. The Gilsman house?' Otis shook his head at the keys.

'How is that building not condemned?! It's damn near falling apart.' Mitch sat clumsily in the red office chair.

'They've tried. Something always winds up tied up in red tape. What happened? Something fell on you?' Otis's grin came and went as Mitch's face took on a stark greyish hue.

'There's something in there with her, no doubt. I saw it.'

'Ain't no way. That lady is alone with a capital A. Just a kook.'

'Otis, I saw it and I heard it. Or them. Something.' 'Saw it how?' Otis sat back in his comfy high-backed office chair. Mitch hadn't noticed how regal it made him look.

'She opened the door,' Mitch said.

'And?' Otis sat, eyes wide.

Mitch rifled through the folders hastily, scattering some contents of Otis's desk to the floor.

'Hey, man! Watch what you're doing!'

'Sorry, Otis. Here!' Mitch pointed to the bright smiling woman in the blue and white tunic.

'Mrs. Gilsman.'

'Yes! But behind that. Don't you see it?!' Mitch pushed his finger into the photo. 'Right there! It's another person or people.'

'I'm not seeing what you're seeing but, maybe she's on the boat with other people. Looks like a vacation photo.'

'But why do we have this photo?' Mitch looked desperately at Otis. 'What's the point? To show her deterioration? That's simple, we could've looked at her driver's license. Something is hovering next to her here.'

Otis took another look. 'Listen. I know this is a tough resident. Been tough since before I took over.' Otis pulled off his ball cap and scratched his head.

'When was that?' Mitch asked.

'2004.'

'Wow. Look, I'm sorry. Not a great first day.' Mitch looked depleted.

'Not something I didn't expect with that route.' Otis stood, circled his desk, and sat on the corner to face Mitch.

'Listen, I wouldn't be begging if we didn't need to retain that route. With Gilsman, set the food on the floor and walk out. She knows it's coming; she'll get it. Ain't nobody gonna try to steal from that place.'

Mitch paled further.

'You want some water?' Otis looked alarmed.

'Just leave it on the ground, huh? Could've told me that earlier.'

Otis jumped up. 'Why? You didn't knock more than once, did you?!'

'Why wouldn't I? I knocked for everyone else.'

'Fair. I should've said.' Otis wiped at his brow. 'Just leave her food next time. No need to go poking bears.'

'Fair.' Mitch stood slowly.

'You sure you're alright?'

'I'll be fine, just a little terrified, no big deal.'

'Ha. If you're sure.'

Mitch staggered to the office door. 'I'm sure. See you next week, Otis.'

'My man!' Otis clapped his hands together. 'Oh hey! Don't forget these!' Otis thrust the folders at Mitch.

'Right.' Mitch couldn't shake the disappointment in his voice. He owed it to Debra to at least make it a few weeks or months before having a 'sit-down' as she liked to call them. He owed it to himself to step out of his comfort zone of always being the cheerleader or leader in general. Now he had a set of marching orders: just leave Gilsman's packages and split. Easy enough. But what about the door? The voices? The whispering? He could've spilled it all and got Otis to change his mind about how stable he was to manage the route.

Otis has to know something along the lines of what I'm talking about, he thought.

Blaming it on the neighborhood seemed odd. Even the kids wouldn't go near the building. And there it was, easy pickings for a hideout or more vandalism. He thought about how he and his childhood friends would run the shit out of that place. Would've been a great place to run away from home when things got hard.

Turning the key into the townhouse door rung hollow that night. Mitch's lips pushed together as they always had when he arrived home, forming the beginnings of the word, 'Babe?' He lowered his shoulders and slinked into the foyer.

The couch, one chair, dining table, and chairs, gone. Everything else remained intact. Mitch turned once about the near-empty living room.

'That couch sucked anyway,' he said out loud.

Still heady from The Gilsman Experiment, he stared blankly into the refrigerator for several minutes before choosing a lager and heading to the upstairs office. He tapped the mousepad of his laptop, booting it out of sleep mode and banged 'Lucy Gilsman' into the search bar and settled in to devour nine pages of results:

- 'Mrs. Lucy Gilsman (19), nee Gifford, married plastics tycoon, Gustavo Gilsman (38) on December 15th, 1956, at 2 pm at St. Francis Church, the reception followed at Belliallo's Country Club, Chautauqua, New York.'
- 'Gilsman marries! Poly-plastics millionaire marries debutante 19 years his junior!'
- 'Lucy Gilsman eyeing the role of Mrs. New York 1960!'
- Work with literacy program sparked her run for the title.'
- 'Gilsman disgraced. Multi-millionaire and new-found spiritualist named profiteer of over 100 tenement properties in Southern Rockland County.'

- 'Lucy Gilsman speaks out against husband's backlash. 'We had no idea.' claims former beauty queen.'
- 'Uproar at Allison Avenue. Domestic dispute turned ugly, Gilsman to serve time.'

'Christ this guy seems like a piece of work.' Mitch shook his beer bottle and grimaced at the lack of contents. He was fixated on an obscure article in Ms. Magazine in 1984 titled, *'Little Girl Lost, The Lucy Gilsman Story.'* He read,

'On all accounts, Lucy Gifford had a fairy tale courtship and wedding to a handsome and charming millionaire. Daughter to a local senator and a librarian, both active in their Catholic church, Lucy was a bubbly blonde who was headed to Wells College in Upstate New York before heading out to a picnic with the dashing tycoon, changing the course of her life.'

A beaming blonde in a bubble flip hairdo waved happily out of a car window.

'As time went on in their marriage, Gustavo exhibited fits of jealousy, whether from Lucy gaining the spotlight or dressing in a way he thought unbecoming. He would demean her in front of guests, friends, and strangers. Several news outlets seemed to salivate at their tumultuous relationship, referring to Lucy as 'The Gilded Girl.' After an abusive outburst, not the first by any means, Gustavo found himself sitting in jail for four months on domestic charges. During this time, Lucy was often seen with his advisor, Lucius McDonald. Lucius had become popular in social circles by incorporating hypnotists and psychics into his decadent parties. He had given the card of one of his favorite seers, Rasmus P., to Gustavo.

Rasmus P. was beloved for his ability to speak to those on the other side, and was said to be able to 'move between the world of the dead and the living.'

'Soul switching,' he coined. Gustavo was fascinated and sought many a private meeting with him, so much so that Rasmus P. had his own small bedroom in their home. A fact that unnerved Lucy. Lucius's constant watch on her during Gustavo's incarceration ensured she couldn't make any plans to leave, get help, or otherwise fend for herself. Towards the end of his time in jail, Lucy could be seen flanked by Lucius and Rasmus P. At women's clothing stores, the country club, anywhere and everywhere. Stationed at her side like two security guards, both Lucius and Rasmus P. were very eager to keep Lucy within harm's way and without any means of refuge. It was rumored that Lucius was ordered to keep Lucy sedated during the day and put to sleep in the evening.

'She was always walking around mumbling to herself. The only time they'd leave her alone was to use the toilet and bathe and even then, they made us stay in the bathroom with her,' claimed former housekeeping staff.

On the day of Gustavo's release, Lucy stood on the steps of her home with the two men and stated how she believed her husband was a changed man, that he'd given up his demons of drinking and anger and they were looking forward to a happy and healthy marriage from this day forward. A speech that former staff said was browbeaten into her and practiced over and over in the days prior until Lucy wept. And as optics would have it, at the close of her speech, Gustavo pulled up to the home, ran up the steps, and pulled Lucy tightly against him in a tearful embrace. Flash, flash, click, click, no more to see here. Months after his release, Lucy Gilsman was only spotted sporadically at certain functions. Her contact with outlets, brief, her contact with family and friends, even more succinct. Where is Lucy Gilsman now? Has she been looked after? Is she still The Gilded Girl? By the records, Lucy Gilsman is very much alive, but who knows for sure?'

The warm-hued image sat ominously at the bottom of the article. A despondent Lucy exiting down the stairs of a private jet, her hair pulled into a low ponytail. Behind her, two men in black suits, one with a grey Fedora and the other, with large, rimmed sunglasses.

'That's gotta be Rasmus P. Fuck. No wonder she went nuts.' Mitch went to close the laptop lid and paused. Lifting it back up he homed in on a familiar entity, the pale face. Only this time, it came attached to a light grey suit.

'Holy shit. Gustavo.' Mitch slammed the laptop shut.

There couldn't be any way that man, that millionaire, would live in such squalor. To be trapped in your own home, your own mind. Mitch felt incredibly guilty. A 'crazy' recluse story carried its own sadness. But being driven to madness altogether was truly tragic.

Whatever was in that apartment, in that building, made her an easy target to stay in that madness. Mitch tried to shake the feeling that Gustavo was still with her somehow. But he was dead. He'd seen the headline, *'Gilsman dead at 84. Fallen tycoon to be buried in Upstate New York.'*

It was a figment after all. Just sad, strange Lucy at the end of a long hall. Making his way into the bathroom, he jumped at the sight of a hot pink post-note:

'Knew you'd see this before bed. Sorry about everything. I've left the ring above the refrigerator in its original box. Maybe we can grab a coffee and talk things out in a few weeks. Love, Christa.'

'Talk what out?' Mitch flipped the toilet seat up, let out the day's business, and flushed. 'I'm leaving it up!' He shouted into the bedroom and chuckled to himself.

Taking lingering looks at the house, a house devoid of noise, devoid of sittable furniture, Mitch smiled. He missed her, of course, and in some strange validation it was nice to know she missed him. But there was something slightly off about the house now. Christa's green sweatshirt, from their first touch football game they attended to meet her family and make it official, hung singularly on her side of the closet. Only one picture frame remained, the cabin deck with Christa sporting her new ring. Mitch took note of his own smile in that picture, one of promise. He felt the corners of his mouth turn down. He was getting angry. Strategic placements of an 'I hope we can put this back together' nature. He'd been here before.

Perhaps that's why this didn't hurt as bad. She'd left twice before. And as soon as he'd begun to live without her, or things began to look up for him socially or financially, she'd swoop back in and cry loneliness. The ride with Christa had been long and hard. And now it was over. And if it was over, he'd need to make a firm boundary, something he was

absolute dogshit at doing with her.

Locking up the front door, his mind turned back to Lucy, The Gilded Girl. A trapped bird. He'd have to tell Debra about it, maybe get a buddy for the route. Maybe find a way to pawn it off. And since he was eating for one, maybe leave the program altogether. He'd have to be secure in saying no to Debra, another thing he was absolute dogshit at.

'An heiress?' Debra pushed her tuna salad around in a container much too big for its contents.

'No, the wife of a plastics tycoon. Gustavo Gilsman. Apparently, the guy was a monster. I read an article about her yesterday. Beaten, drugged, hovered over, just terrible. I feel for her.'

'Tycoon makes her sound rich. How'd she end up in Jackson?'

'Beats me. My only guess is that it's one of the old man's tenement properties he got in trouble for decades ago. Can't keep her locked up after you die unless you put her where no one's gonna look for her.' Mitch stood and stretched and turned an ear to a slightly raised voice in the hallway. Olivia trying to reason with resident streaker Mr. Fitzsimmons again.

'Wow. You seem pretty invested already.' Debra put her container aside and checked her computer screen quizzically. 'Well, this might give us a clue.' Debra turned her screen to Mitch. 'Looks like his will left everything to a person named Rasmus P. or Rasmus P. Dunne except a small stipend for Mrs. Gilsman's furnishings.'

Mitch leaned in. 'Figures. How small? That place is falling apart.'

'I know. It's so sad. Now I'm bummed. Maybe I can arrange for a few extra things to be put in, blankets, soap, books, something.'

'Debra, how did she end up on the route anyway?'

'Lemme see. Windsong Inc.'s database has everything from what they ate today to the clothes they were buried in.' Debra clicked away. 'Looks like she was originally moved to The Cottages at Northwoods upstate in 2000 from a private residence in Chautauqua, New York soon after her husband passed.'

'Why couldn't she just be free at home? That's an active adult facility, right? What happened? Natural decline?' Mitch spun around Debra's desk moving the screen with him.

'It looks like she was quite the go-getter there. She spearheaded a ladies' knitting circle and movie night as well as a photography group.'

'Alright, Lucy!' Mitch clapped to himself, stopping abruptly at the side-eye from Debra.

'This is odd. Seems that she was beginning a memoir with a woman named MaryAnne Folger when she was pulled from The Cottages in 2002 and sent to Pineview Rehabilitation Facility in Pearl Harbor, New York.'

'The psychiatric hospital?! Why?'

'I'm reading just like you, Mitch.'

'Sorry.' Mitch stood back a little and for a moment could not figure out what to do with his hands. Lucy was being tormented from beyond the grave, still just as watched, fussed, and mishandled as she'd always been.

'She remained at Pineview for seven months before returning to The Cottages in 2003. A complete 180. Mostly non-responsive yet not catatonic. Healthy appetite but mostly had conversations with herself. She left The Cottages under the care of a Mr. Lucius McDonald, Mr. Gilsman's power of attorney, and became a dependent on the Operation Icebox program the following year.'

'Fuck me.' Mitch stared suspiciously at the screen.

'Excuse me?' Debra sat back amazed.

'Sorry, Debra, but this is just awful. Hang on. Any note of who pulled her out of The Cottages to begin with?'

'Hmm.' Deb began to click again. 'Fuck me.'

'Debra!'

A shared laugh was cut short by the name on the screen.

'Mr. Lucius McDonald. Mitch, I'm getting a little confused here. Who are these people?'

'Based on what I read, the same guys her husband had keep watch of her when he was in prison for abusing her. Makes sense that they would stay on the payroll. Looks like as soon as she started telling her side of the story—' Mitch straightened quickly. 'Debra, what was that woman's name that was writing her memoir?'

Debra scoured the computer screen. 'Uh, MaryAnne Folger.'

Mitch furiously typed her name into his phone. His eyes closed tightly.

'She's dead.'

Debra gasped. 'How long?'

'Since 2002. Car accident.'

Debra covered her mouth and closed the tab on the computer.

'Mitch, I'm not sure what we're dealing with here but I'm going to ask you, as hard as it is, to keep this under wraps and keep the status quo. Deliver the packages and that's it. No more digging. These people sound dangerous and if they've got an inkling we're putting things together . . . ' Debra looked incredibly stressed and pinched the top of her nose with her fingers.

'Debra,' Mitch almost whispered.

'Mitch, please. Please don't go hunting around. Stay safe and on the task. And get the hell out of here, it's past five.'

Mitch heaved a sigh that encompassed the entire room. 'Alright. See you tomorrow.'

He'd let himself down. Instead of getting out of the Icebox game entirely, he'd gone and plunged himself into *Lucy Gilsman: The Miniseries.* He'd fought for patient's rights his entire career. For their safety and security. He was letting Lucy down by not being anywhere near providing either one. And apparently, some folks still liked it that way. Folks that had to be getting up there in age themselves. He thought about Lucius and Rasmus P. all the way home. The size and orchestration of their little operation. How far ahead they'd planned Lucy's life before Gustavo died.

She was just a kid when he picked her out of a sea of undergrads and stunted her just as quickly as he married her.

What was he saying? Or feeling? Lucy was getting under his skin. It was time to know what he knew and just be happy with that. A poor woman fell through the cracks and as long as he could provide her with food and necessities, he should be happy with that. A sad story yes, but not his to right or solve. Yet.

Leave it alone, Mitch.

Mitch entered the foyer to a pink gift bag adorned with three helium-filled heart balloons.

'Honestly.' He fussed with the small envelope attached to the bag and jostled out the card.

'Wanted to say congrats on the new job! So happy you're moving up in the world! Saw this and immediately thought of you. Enjoy! My new book club meets at Copper's on Tuesdays if you ever wanna grab a drink after work. Love Christa.'

Rustling into the gift bag, he emerged with a Chewbacca beer stein. The very same one he thought was hilarious at Spencer's and was told how impractical it was and how it wouldn't go with the kitchenware. But now it was just perfect. Supposing it was, considering she wouldn't be there to stare at it. It was all getting a bit ridiculous, but this was the old song and dance they'd gone through several times. She wanted out, then back in, then out.

Mitch placed it on the table, grabbed his keys, and took the bag out to the back trash cans. Putting the final screws in the new lock sets, Mitch felt safe in his home for the first time since Christa's hot pink post-it. There was an odd boldness this time, creeping back into the house to leave whatever or take whatever.

He'd leave a set with Mr. Calaree tomorrow and explain the situation. He would spend this weekend re-furnishing.

'Mrs. Gilsman's Furnishings.' he thought.

He'd now spend nights watching TV shows only he had an interest in. Sleeping late for a change and not meeting Christa's mother every Saturday at 8am at the $17 latte place. It was all going to be forward movement from this point. He took a look at the backyard stretching across the horizon. He did like it out here, even though he originally protested. Falling leaves began to thin out the trees and the deer couldn't hide as well between them. At least ten of them mingled around one spot. Circling the smallest of them. A sign of promise. One of Christa's persuasion balloons had gotten free of the trash lid and waved errantly about the receptacle, ruining the earnest nature shot he'd been enjoying. He decided to keep the blinds closed for a while.

It had been a pleasurable weekend alone and now the house felt more like him. A love seat and a nice wide recliner for him. A long coffee table with excellent first editions he'd hidden away. A high-top, butcher block four-seater for a dining set. The blinds remained closed. Thick down bedspread in the gorgeous hunter green he adored. All was right as Monday and Tuesday swung by with ease in both EverGreen 'steps.'

'You ready for another round?' Otis laughed and handed Mitch the yellow ribboned keys of destiny.

'I think so. I was reading up on her last week. Sad story. Her husband . . . '

'I know, I know. Real shitbag.'

Mitch stepped back on his heel, miffed at being robbed of delivering Lucy's story.

'Just leave the packages at the door.'

'I know, I know. No knocking.'

'My man!' Otis patted him on the shoulder. 'See you soon, Amherst.'

'Ha! You got it.'

The apartment building loomed large with angst against the musky orange sky. He'd gotten the new neighborhood lowdown from Ms. Jones. Mr. Finney was knuckle-deep in another dated porno and shouted for the packages to be left on the ground. Ms. Baum tried to give him two dollars this time.

'Just leave them, no knocking. Just leave them, no knocking.' He thought repeatedly.

A pool of sweat had already made a home in his lower back as he entered the caution-filled hallway. A second look at the crude graffiti made Mitch feel terrible. These people had no idea about her, about what she'd gone through to end up here. Or maybe they did and didn't care to learn anything further. She'd gone mad as a March Hare and just had to sit there and take it.

A brief high-pitched whine caught his ear, snapping him out of his silent campaign for Lucy's good name. Panicked, he'd dropped the dairy tote. Again. He winced and prepared his brain for the assault, but all that came was a soft blow of a trumpet. Quickly gathering the tote, he pushed forward from the dilapidated staircase to see the door to 10A was ajar.

'Just leave them, no knocking. Just leave them, no knocking.' Hell of a good plan now. Surely someone would see him, or come to assist or at any rate, or pull a Mr. St. James and just watch him struggle. His feet carried him abruptly to the front door of 10A. He was drooling. For how long? Had he forgotten how to swallow? A puff of white gathered near the door frame.

'Hello.'

Mitch dropped everything and watched as items rolled and scattered in slow motion.

'Oh my God! I'm so sorry.' Mitch began to pant and quickly

gathered the dairy pieces and vegetables. A bag of pasta had broken, and a large potato had rolled behind the curve of the banister. He didn't dare turn his back on her to retrieve it.

'Leave it. I'll get it later.' The infamous Lucy Gilsman stood in a blue housedress and brown slippers, hair wild, but some semblance of a cotton candy wisp tightly tied in a low ponytail at the base of her neck.

Mitch looked up sorrowfully. 'I really am sorry.'

Her deep-set brown eyes were bewildering. Part dancing, part anguish.

'No bother. Come in, come in.'

Lucy led and Mitch quietly followed into her tight but well-kept apartment. Stately and well-curated pieces, table statues, clawfoot furniture. A strange juxtaposition to the well-worn brown Berber wall-to-wall carpet. Mitch set the packages down near an end table with a full view of the kitchen but went no further. He looked at the door.

'Would you like me to close this, Mrs. Gilsman?'

Lucy's hands shot up in fear. 'No, no! I'm expecting someone and I want to make sure I hear them when they come back. And, Lucy, please. Mitch is it?'

Mitch stepped back. 'Yes, how did you know?'

'Is it not Wednesday? You said you'd be back.'

Mitch smiled. 'It is, Lucy. Well, you've got the Shepherd's Pie Package today and all but the escaped potato outside, you should have everything you need to make quite a nice...'

Mitch's eyes fell upon a frame on the end table. Gustavo and Lucy's wedding photo.

Lucy's face scowled.

'My late husband and I. Has to be gosh, over fifty years ago now.'

Mitch's heart rate galloped. Lucy's round teenage face against the thin, pale one of Gustavo's was like a yin and yang. His jet-black hair so close to her pale blonde strands made the contrast even more somber. Such differences right from the start.

'Well, you look very pretty here.' Mitch swallowed hard.

'I look very pretty now.' Lucy let out a small chuckle and Mitch followed suit.

'Uh, as I said Ms., uh, Lucy, you should be all stocked 'til next week.'

'Oh please, sit. Been such a long time since I had a visitor.'

'I thought you said you were expecting someone.'

'Mitch, do you like Herb Alpert? Oh!' She put her hand to her chest. 'How I used to flit around my house to Herb Alpert and the Tijuana Brass. The parties we used to have. Such a nice time.'

Mitch sat down in the chair next to Lucy, no couch to be found. 'I think it sounds fine, Lucy. Very warm.'

'You know I've said that too? Can't feel bad listening to this.'

Mitch sat forward and watched as Lucy's smile gained power. She closed her eyes and let her hands dance about the air around her.

'Lucy?'

'Mmhmm?' Eyes closed.

'Lucy, I was wondering, well, I was reading about you a few days ago and I find you very interesting. I was hoping I could talk to you about your life a little, if I could.'

'Ha! My life a little. A little life.' Lucy's smile faded. 'What would you like to know Mitch?'

Mitch licked his lips, fervent with questions. Who were Lucius and Rasmus P.? What happened after you left The Cottages? What happened when Gustavo was in jail?

'What made you marry Gustavo?' He winced at his bad choice of a leadoff question.

Lucy let out a raucous laugh. 'Well, Mitch, when you are the only girl to a God-fearing man, you do what Daddy tells you.'

'But you were just a kid!' Mitch sat back, embarrassed. 'Sorry.'

'Don't apologize. I was a kid who was going to promote literacy in foreign countries. I was going to go to Wells and then travel the world. My father told me that was un-American. I had a duty to help children here. I reluctantly agreed and decided to change my track to elementary education. Until my father, who had designs on real estate to support his gambling habit and my mother's gin habit, ran into Gustavo Gilsman at a Moose Club luncheon. Gustavo was speaking. My father fell in love. Gustavo was the man he wanted to be. Solid, rich, thin, charismatic, bold. My father stood all of five foot eight and was about as wide as he was tall. He was showing Gussy pictures of me and my mother in his pontoon boat. Gussy settled on my picture and said he'd like to meet me under the guise of providing scholarship money for college. Which of course my father jumped at. It wasn't just the social standing of being personally championed by Gussy, but the fact that his daughter was someone's future he believed in. My father was never more kind in all his life than the week before I met Gussy.'

Mitch couldn't believe how soft, kind, and lucid Lucy seemed. Relying mostly on an exposé and wall graffiti, Mitch was disappointed in himself at how he viewed her. He sat with his chin pressed into his hand, just listening.

'So, was it love at first sight?'

'Hardly. My father introduced me, and Gussy and I chatted about poverty, the plight of the homeless, and illiteracy and he had a counterargument for everything. Instantly, I despised him, and like a good little girl, ate my catered Chicken Françoise without a fuss. My father and Gussy headed to the study for Cognac, in the middle of the day mind you, and my mother dragged me into the kitchen by the skin of my arm.'

'Hell of a fix-up.' Mitch laughed.

'You're telling me. 'He's a very nice man, and you've disrespected him by being so ornery,' she told me, to which I relented because the sooner that man stepped out of my house I wouldn't have to entertain him any longer. Later my father emerged with Gussy and they gathered us around our coffee table in the parlor. Gussy introduced my father as his new partner in the Felix-Hammer Strip Mall project. My mother's palms almost lost their skin she clapped so hard.'

Mitch howled in laughter and caught himself.

'And then Gussy said to me, 'Young lady, I have to deeply apologize. If you hadn't noticed, I was being quite contrary on purpose, you'll forgive me. A girl with such strong stances will always be asked to defend them, and my dear I'm very impressed.' Well, I don't know what got into me, but I grew quite fond of Gussy myself after that.'

'Aww no! You fell for it?' Mitch recoiled.

'Hook, line, and sinker. I ditched Wells and became his wife six months later, and we had the most glorious first three years of any marriage I'd ever known. Until he met Lucius.'

'I've heard about him.' Mitch grimaced. 'Um, when I read a bit about you, about all the folks on my route.'

He was stammering, desperately trying to save his eager, meddling face.

'Hmm. Most have. Lucius was a hanger-on to the wealthy. Always putting stock tips in their ears, vacation ideas, and business ideas. Pretty soon he was seen as a master forecaster for all things the rich could burn their money on. Gussy loved him. He made Gussy eight-hundred thousand the first month they'd been friends. Well, that's all he needed to know. Gussy put him on the payroll and would 'loan' him out to his friends. He became a coveted and hard-to-attain source. Gussy loved that. He'd found a rare resource, and folks would do anything to get in good. That's when the parties began. Gussy would plan these lavish pool parties in the summer and then fireplace parties in the fall and winter, inviting all of the who's who. He'd give folks fifteen minutes with Lucius for a thousand dollars a pop; the parties paid for themselves.'

'Wild.' Mitch took quick stock of the fact that he'd pulled his knees to his chest on the chair, eager to hear what came next. He slowly extended his legs and tried in vain to play it cool and get back to a normal sitting position.

'Is that where Rasmus P. came in?' Lucy shot him a wild look. Mitch's mouth hung open, dry. 'Oh God, I'm sorry.'

Lucy put her hand up. 'It's alright. I just don't speak that name in my home. That man has done and gotten done the evilest things and I don't want to give him any more credit.'

'Understood.'

'But yes, that's when he came into the fold. Lucius had brought him to a party once, I think, to take the attention off himself. He'd given a series of bad tax advice and was dodging a few of the heavy hitters who'd lost their shirts. Gussy was very defensive of Lucius and would simply pay them what they'd lost. No harm, no foul. That man, I'll call him, did a string of psychic questions to the audience which they devoured, most were partially true but that was enough. How Gussy had managed to partner with the most slimy, untalented duo I'll never know. But that man came to every party after that. He began pulling Gussy aside, psychic business advice and forecasting, speaking to his dead mother from beyond the grave, things like that. Gussy came to rely on him so heavily that he'd given him a room in our home. The way I protested; I was a beast. We were never alone. It was always either that man or the other one. I had no time privately with my husband anymore.' Lucy swallowed. 'And that's when the hitting started.'

'Lucy I'm so sorry. He did get arrested eventually, right?' Mitch's legs had crept back up the chair.

Lucy snorted. 'All the good that did. Heckle and Jeckle watched me day and night. I spent most of the year going in and out of consciousness and they told me if I talked to the press or had any designs on leaving, Gussy would paint me as a drug addict and deviant who couldn't be trusted. Even my mother turned me away when I finally found the courage to sneak off in the middle of the night. 'Ungrateful and ungodly to leave a man when he's down.' she said. Down, for beating her daughter. So, Gussy had won this round, and at home I stayed. Gussy would tell me that he'd rather see me dead than away from him. No one was gonna have me but him, no way, no how.'

Mitch had been wringing his hands so hard they burned.

'Gussy had been distraught in his last years. That man had traveled to Portugal, on Gussy's dime of course, to learn some sort of series of rituals to ensure eternal life. He hadn't returned or hadn't called until one day in November he showed up on our doorstep, looking like a shepherd.' Lucy let out a little laugh. 'He'd found it.'

'Found what?'

'The key to eternal life.' Lucy's air quotes danced on bony fingers.

'So, he says.'

'That's what I thought too.' Lucy's brow furrowed heavily. 'Gussy died that year. I had no energy to fight Lucius and the law firm. That man took ninety percent of Gussy's assets including my home, Gussy's car, and fifty percent share in all of his businesses. Lucius had been getting a handsome stipend for years that he'd been investing and squirreling away. And me, I was moved to an old folk's home with just enough to cover my monthly bill.'

A small clamor erupted in the hallway. Lucy shot up from her chair.

'You have to go. My, my guest is coming.'

'Lucy, I'm not leaving you here alone.'

'Please, Mitch, he cannot find you here.'

'Who?!'

'Mitch, please!' Lucy pushed him towards the door. Mitch swiftly turned around and grabbed her harder than he meant to, and she flinched.

'Lucy who is coming?'

Lucy softened in his arms. 'Gussy.' She whispered. 'Gussy's not dead, he's never been dead. And he won't leave me alone. No one can have me. No one can help me. Now, please. Go.'

Mitch let go gently and grabbed hold of his head tightly. The din had returned, so strong Mitch's ears began to bleed. His scream blended with Lucy's as a long black shadow fell into the room. Mitch's body shot across the room, knocking into the closet door. His head spun as he slowly lifted his gaze. A long-fingered figure stood looming over Lucy who hovered a foot in the air over her chair.

'Leave her alone!' Mitch shouted.

The figure turned, pulling an unnatural sound out of Mitch. It scattered on crude legs that looked like bone spindles. Dropping Lucy hard to the floor, its bones cracked and popped as it scurried like a spider over to Mitch. Its long, pale face dragged along the floor and the jaw of its massive head became unhinged.

'You cannot have her!' It hissed. Tendrils of white ooze dripped from its many sharp teeth. 'She is mine!'

'Let her go!'

The figure snapped a bony spindle at Mitch, deeply cutting his cheek. Another pierced into his leg sending him crying out to Lucy.

Lucy bent over the figure with a tall lamp.

'Gussy stop!' She swung down hard, dazing the monster. 'Mitch go! Now!'

'Lucy! I can't leave you like this!'

'I've been fighting this all my life. Go!'

'I'm coming back with help!'

'Don't ever do that. Go!'

Mitch limped to the door and stepped out, turning to Lucy who was bound tightly by the bony spindles of the Gussy. The figure squeezed as Lucy stood, wide-eyed, nearly catatonic. Mitch stared harder at the spindles as they pulsed in the room. They became fluid, clear, and unremarkable to the eye. A large roar erupted in the hallway as all the voices returned and the wet whisper of Gussy rang into Lucy's ear. It had been there before. Last week. He was seeing it in its full glory this time. Lucy's cage would never go away. She would never be free. He lumbered to the van and almost fell forward at the sight of a long-haired elderly man.

'Those kids are really quite a pair aren't they?' A low, fluid Southern drawl crawled out of his mouth that had too many teeth to make sense. The man walked forward. 'Rasmus P. Dunne Esq. You look like you require a little help, son.'

'You sonofabitch! Did you do that? Did you make that monster?! He's gonna kill her!'

Rasmus sucked at his teeth. 'Don't you think he would've done that in all the years he's had? I will say it does get a little tiring wrangling him in after one of these episodes.'

'How can you be so smug? This is insane!'

'What's insane is you can't seem to leave well enough alone. But to your impatient point and what look to be time-sensitive wounds, I'm willing to put an end to the old girl's suffering. Enough is enough and I've got better things to do than to follow this Geist around. We can't be letting the secret out, can we? I mean look at you.'

'Fuck you!' Mitch collapsed face down on the concrete walkway.

A pinhole of bright light gave him a shudder down his spine.

'Mr. Monahan?'

Mitch blinked.

'Hello, Mr. Monahan! I'm Erica. How're we feeling?'

'What?' Mitch tried to turn on his side and exhaled heavily 'Oh God.'

'Slowly Mr. Monahan. You've been through quite a lot.'

'You could say that.'

'An older gentleman brought you in and said he'd seen you attacked by a loose dog. Just awful, he said no one would help you.'

'Did he have a name?'

'No, he didn't leave one. But it looks like you're good to go home. Now, you've got five stitches in your cheek, they may drain so keep it clean. A few bruised ribs but no breakage and you've got twenty-nine stitches in this leg. It's packed with gauze. Leave it tonight and then change every four hours from here on out.'

'Alright.'

Erica helped Mitch sit up.

'Any dizziness?'

'Nope, just a hell of a headache.' He reached into his back pocket, no cellphone.

'It's over here in your effects, Mr. Monahan.' Erica shook a white plastic bag titled 'Patient Clothing".'

'Oh good. I'll need an Uber.' He stood and dug around for his phone. Three missed calls from Otis and fourteen from Christa. He wondered if he should ask to be admitted.

As the Uber pulled up to the Operation Icebox parking lot, it seemed dismal and abandoned. It had just turned 9 pm. Otis was gone, but his lone little red Traxx stood singularly in the parking lot. Mitch thanked the driver and limped laboriously with one crutch to the garage. He peered through the glass of the garage doors. One, two, three, four, five. All vans returned. How, he didn't know, or care. He needed sleep. And a beer. A beer and sleep. He would tell Debra about the 'dog' and turn in his Operation Icebox Director folders on Friday. He'd need to take the day off tomorrow. Rasmus was right. He couldn't leave well enough alone.

He pulled into parking space four at Windy Meadows Townhomes to see Mr. Calaree's green Suburban in space five, idling. Shifting out of the car, Mitch came around to the driver's side to greet Mr. Calaree. Mr. Calaree spilled lazily out of his Suburban.

'Wow, you look like shit!'

'Yeah, I had a little accident.'

'Sorry to hear that.'

'Everything okay Mr. Calaree?'

'It is now, but that little girlfriend of yours . . . '

'She's not my girlfriend anymore, Mr. Calaree.'

'Well, whatever the hell you two got going on, it needs to calm down. She came ranting into my office that you'd changed the locks, which you're not supposed to do, but encountering her today I see why you did. She had a gift for you and demanded to be let in. I said I could let her in to drop it off and that's it, or she could leave it with me, and I'd get it to you. Then it turned into you've got something she asked for and she doesn't wanna have to call the sheriff's department to help her come down and get it. And at that,

I'd had enough. So, we went in and she started tearing through the apartment, running from room to room. And she came running out with an armful of things and a stack of papers. I'm sorry I didn't wanna get in her way. She left with tears in her eyes. I did tell the sheriff's department that I'd be calling them the next time she shows up.'

Mitch sighed heavily.

'I know it's a lot. And you look like hell. Just wanted to give you a heads up.'

'I appreciate it Mr. Calaree.'

'Well, goodnight.'

'Goodnight, Mr. Calaree.'

'Oh! And whoever this new Lucy woman is that she was raving about, tell her she better watch out. That woman is on a mission.' Mr. Calaree pulled away.

Mitch entered the home with a thud as the door bounced back on his leg. Nothing in the home looked amiss. Finally opening all his calls from this afternoon, he opened the call history to Otis. He answered on the first ring.

'What the hell happened to you today?!' Otis screamed into the phone.

'Otis, it's a very long story.'

'You sound terrible, you alright? We went looking for the van when you didn't come back at one and found it on Hockaborne Way. One of the neighborhood boys says you came running out of there bloody. She attack you?'

'No, no not at all. I left the packages by the door and there was an angry dog in there. Someone must've left the front door open, and he wandered in. Pretty chewed up, no rabies though. Sorry about that, Otis.'

Christ that's alright. I'll let Debra know, no need to hash it out to her again. Rest up.' 'Yeah, I'm gonna need it.'

'I bet. Good to hear you're alright.'

'For the most part. Goodnight Otis.'

'Alright man.'

Dial tone.

Fourteen messages from Christa. He'd been here before. Just listen to the last one, no need to follow the escalation.

'Listen you asshole, if you wanna ignore me that's fine but

you're not gonna make a fool out of me. Who the fuck is Lucy? There's notes and scribbles all over this house about her and yes, I'm in OUR house. I'm gonna prove you've been fucking her since day one and I'm taking this house back; do you hear me? We just broke up and you're pulling this? It's sick. You never cared about us. Well, I'm gonna find this Lucy and tell her the exact kind of person you are, see if she's still interested.'

A large rustle of papers scratched through the phone.

'13 Hockeborne Way in Jackson. Slumming, I see. Interesting. Have a good night, Mitch.'

The grace about cellphones was that you couldn't slam the phone anymore, making whatever gestures or expletive-ridden rants pretty anticlimactic, but a thought ran through him. He couldn't let Christa encounter Gussy.

Mitch hobbled to the front door and did his best to rush to the car. Back to Hockeborne Way he'd go. A low hum from his phone on the car seat caught his attention as he sped through the streets of Willis heading to Jackson. Otis.

'Hey, Otis, what's going on?'

'Are you sitting down?'

'I'm driving so, yeah I guess.'

'I'm sorry to tell you this but, Lucy Gilsman is dead.'

Mitch slammed on the brakes and pulled to the side of the road.

'What? What happened?!'

'Looks like the building collapsed. The fire department had no idea there were any residents still there even though there was still power to the building. She was crushed to death. Mitch, I'm so sorry. I know she was a tough one, but I know you cared.'

'That's um..' Mitch began to cry. 'That's okay Otis, that place was bound to fall sooner or later. That's very sad. I, uh, I'll see if there's anywhere to pay respects in a few days.'

'Alright man, again, really sorry.'

'Thanks for letting me know, Otis.'

Mitch pressed end and sat slumped over the steering wheel. Poor Lucy. Her whole life had been a hard one. Bound and trapped by jealousy and spite. Her husband turning himself into some evil monster to keep her a prisoner. Perhaps this was Rasmus P. showing mercy. A killing that couldn't be traced. He was almost grateful that she had gone out of her misery. The Gilded Girl was free; her cage had fallen.

Christa.

Christa had gone to Lucy's out of anger. She could be trapped too. Mitch pushed back into gear swiftly towards Jackson. Several city workers were barricading the remaining structure with bright orange gating. No sign of Christa's blue Jeep, or any cars for that matter. Dust permeated the sky, casting the corpse of the building in a tan haze.

'If it's any consolation . . . ' Mitch swung around to see Rasmus P. 'I put her to sleep before we detonated. Never felt a thing.'

Mitch couldn't speak. He was angry, sad, and bewildered. Touched. He cleared his throat heartily.

'Was anyone else in the building?'

'You mean that pretty little brunette? Yeah, she was banging on the door and screaming filth on your name. Dear, dear, Mitch, what have you done to that woman?'

'Did she talk to Lucy?'

'No. I did meet her inside to tell her that the building was condemned years ago. She didn't like the sound of that.'

'And she left?'

'Eventually. A little shaken, but yes. Scooted away in her truck, looked expensive.'

'It is. And what of Gustavo?'

Rasmus P. sighed. 'He didn't like the idea of letting go but we made a little arrangement where he could take all that furious anger and direct it elsewhere. Talk about clingy.'

'And what about you?' Mitch cried silently. He didn't know what to make of things, of life, of his decision to take this route. Why couldn't he leave well enough alone?

'I am going to take a long vacation someplace warm and undisturbed.' Rasmus P. tipped his large sunglasses to Mitch. 'I wish you good health and energy, Mitchell Monahan. You're gonna need it.'

Rasmus P. began to walk gently down Hockaborne Way, turning the corner at Tall Avenue and was out of sight.

He waited as the spring hinge front door of the townhouse swung back, holding it with his hands so it didn't bump his leg this time. It was all a wash. His whole life, his whole career. It *was* a dead-end industry. One woman was dead. He, almost dead. One man, dead a long time. Maybe it was time to get on the insurance gig. To make amends.

He locked the door behind him and a long hiss in his head dropped him to his knees.

The click-clack of bone on low-middle-class linoleum floor. The spindles slipped along the four stairs up to the living room. Mitch screamed as the pale face came into light, a round soft face he could place anywhere.

'Hello, lover. Miss me?' The jaw of Christa's round face unhinged wide, exposing teeth of all sizes and wetness. Mitch crouched by the door. Her voice gargled with a white ooze that trailed along the floor.

'So glad to be home. And I'm never gonna leave you again.'

'Christa, please.' Mitch whimpered. A long tongue lashed against his cheek, licking at his tears.

'Oh, babe, no. We can be together forever from now on. I won't leave you and you won't ever leave me.'

Mitch lay against the floor cradled in two of her spindles.

'You left me first.' Mitch swung up with car keys still in hand and plunged the icicle-shaped glass breaker into his own heart.

Christa's new figure pulsed and scratched at the floor with all of its spindles. It thrashed and screeched loudly. Throwing its head back, her eye came down hard onto the glass breaker handle. The spindles twitched, scattered wildly and then slowed. And there they lay. Two lovers. As if they never parted at all.

13
DEATH

I WISH I COULD GROW PLANTS

HAVE A black thumb, I think.

Everything I touch turns to coal or something like that. But I suppose that's just as well because more often than not, I can't keep things alive anyway. Not my fish, not my dog, Francie, not my succulent I got at the county fair. Who kills a succulent? You've got to be joking. Not my teeny spider plant that never grew enough to curl over the pot before turning brown. Not my parents and not I.

Yes. I understand death and what it means, and I am well aware that you won't see this until later but it's like a release in some sort of way. It's necessary. Death and this entry respectively, I guess.

I couldn't grow plants, but I could see things coming. Awful things. Terrible things.

Haunting things.

And I see it all coming for them. For Margie, my mother, with brown hair that curls under her ear naturally, from decades of it being pulled that way. Curtis, my father, whose left eyebrow conceals a star-shaped birthmark. He once told me he was 'born magical'. Whatever was coming, it was coming to swallow up all the magic in the room, in the house, on the block.

It will be gruesome, and it will be fast. And so, I place all my things in strategic places. My diary will sit on my bed, askew. My laundry is in piles about the room. I'll pull down the rod in my closet and perch it at an angle. Messy. Broken. I'll go downstairs where the smell of my mom's pot roast hangs in the air. My dad will read the paper at the head of the table as usual. I'll fling my arms around his neck, my hands laying gently on his chest, and ask what he's reading.

'The End of Days!' He'll exclaim, and something within me will tense.

He'll pat my arm and laugh. 'The Rams lost again last night.' I'll kiss him on his head and glide over to my mother, whose head hangs down looking into the simmer pot she's stirring like a mad scientist. The kitchen window light of dusk will circle her head like a halo. My stomach will turn. I'll put my chin on her shoulder, and she'll smile.

'Mmmm,' Is all I can muster.

And I feel terrible. My mother blushes ten shades of red at every present she gets. A woman whose faith in God has never wavered, even through all of my father's low- hanging skepticism.

'I'm going to finish that report before dinner,' I say, and I slink out of the kitchen.

'Ten minutes!' My mother shouts after me and my stomach turns again.

How does she know? How does she know she only has ten minutes? Ten minutes before a maniac walks blithely out of the woods behind our home and boldly through our back door? Ten minutes before an axe drives straight through my father's skull, drenching the sports page, and exactly ten minutes and twenty-seven seconds before her head falls sloppily into her pot roast supper.

Or, ten minutes until a gang of roughnecks break into our home and terrorize and beat my father and tie him, gagged, to the dining room chair and make him watch as they dismember my mother.

Or ten minutes until my father gasps loudly and falls backwards of a heart attack and my mother in her haste to run to him trips on the kitchen rug and falls headlong into the marble kitchen island, cracking her skull.

We've gone through all of this before. Every day. Every day since the brownout last summer, where the heat got so intense, it threw me into my very first seizure. And that's when the black thumb began. So, most days we die. Again, and again.

The furrow on my father's brow as I come down in a cropped top too high for his liking lets me know that today is maniac day and today is where it all stops. I've been searching for a connecting thread, a what happens when, a this and then that for the last 356 days. Today I stop the wheel.

I quicken my pace from the kitchen to my bedroom and

dishevel my room. If I push my dresser drawers out just right, I can curl my body in the spaces behind it. The carpet is soft and plush, and I can drag it back towards me with ease. A lesson my mother taught me, a lesson to destroy my father at hide and go seek. And I wait. And I breathe. And then it starts.

Mom screams. There is a choked sound. A half-snatched holler. A grunt.

Footsteps on the stairs. The banging of doors so hard, the knobs break through the sheetrock. He's there. In my room. He walks purposefully over to the closet and makes a racket. Tossing things this way and that. And then there is silence. He's not moving. He's listening. And he listens for what seems like forever.

Time is funny; it flies during fun and drags along miserably when you want to move, to run. But in that sliver of time, all you want is more. More time to get away. More time to live. And I will live.

He finally moves out of my room, and I hear him stumbling blindly, searching for something. It doesn't sound like he knows what.

And I wait. I'm not moving. I'm listening. I unfurl myself and half crawl, half slither to my bed. There's a small Louisville Slugger between my nightstand and bed that I palm. I head downstairs and the front door lingers open. The screen door sways gently with the night breeze. I tighten my grip around the bat.

I turn at the bottom and see the headless body of my mother lying in a position only meant for a dropped doll. I lurch and I notice that I am not crying. I've seen this movie before. Asleep. Awake. I've watched it all from start to finish.

Some days, we eat the pot roast dinner happily and I lovingly chide my dad about his bad dance moves, or he pokes fun at my mother's sensitivity when it comes to sad movies. Sometimes they live. Most times they don't.

Most times they die.

But I understand in this moment that the black thumb is real. The sully hand that makes a mark, a mark of death. A wrinkle in time that changes everything. And I've written this all down in the diary I've left, in a haphazard drop, on my bed, that's been scribbled in for the past year.

Every word. Every step.

I wish I could take it all back. I wish I wasn't this way. I wish Francie didn't die after I'd held her all night long. If I didn't hold her so long, she wouldn't have run out to the road. If I hadn't put the fishbowl on the windowsill on the hottest day, Freddy Mercury, the fish, would still be with us. My succulent, the spider plant. They would all be thriving. Pulsing. Alive.

I wish I could grow plants.

I wish I could've just come to dinner and not touched my parents.

I wish I'd never come downstairs, where he waited on the front porch to slaughter me too. I always forget that possibility. I always forget.

6

THE LOVERS

DANDELION WINE

JOYCE AND JERRY BOYD from Ocean City, New Jersey, had just won a plum cake from the church bingo game the day before Halloween. Joyce kept on about, 'slicing this baby up with some coffee.' Jerry wanted the lawn mower. The RH-80 Red Push Mower with a removable bag. Damn Ghendersons. They weren't even supposed to come, let alone bring Dixie Ghenderson's mother. It threw off the whole balance, Jerry thought. Threw it off entirely.

Twenty-two people enter that hall on the last Sunday of every month. Twenty-two. Today it tipped the scales at twenty-seven. Odd number. More cards, more chances to spread the wealth. He could see it now, Sam Ghenderson's fat hand waving to him from over the fence, sporting his new lawn mower. Jerry couldn't stomach it. He revved the engine home.

'Jesus! You want me to drop this?' Joyce screamed.

'Can it! Can you believe those guys? Sonsabitches.'

'The church bingo is a free country, Jerry. There's no assigned seating.'

'Well, if you hadn't had to be so neighborly and tell them about it.' Jerry re-gripped the steering wheel in anger.

'It would do you good to be a little neighborly occasionally. You always act like a jerk when you don't win what you want. Last month it was the Curtis's fault you didn't get the turkey roaster, and before that, it was the Clark's fault for you not getting the garden hose attachments. When's it gonna end? Maybe we should just stop going!'

Jerry slammed on the brakes, thrusting the entire cake into the dash, sending Joyce tucking it to her bust. Joyce's eyes widened. Jerry pushed the car slowly back in gear, terrified. Now he'd done it. It wasn't a scream Joyce was after, nor a fight to the death. It was pure silence. And she was dead good at it.

Entering the home, two hands still carrying the glass cake plate, Joyce placed it neatly on the counter and washed her hands. She stripped off her clothing in the kitchen down to her slip dress, which was unharmed, and threw her dress and stockings in the trash without any pomp or circumstance. She pulled the seven pins out of her hair and laid them on the kitchen counter; she shook her hair gently and headed upstairs to the bathroom. The shower wheezed then rang out a light pour of water.

Jerry sat on the edge of the loveseat watching the entire show in agony. He had hoped for a fight, or at least a snide remark got in edgewise, but nothing. As usual. Joyce's game was letting it fester, then bringing it back up in front of company six months to two years down the road.

'Poor Joyce', they'd all say.

'What a good Samaritan to stay married to that oaf.'

It wasn't untrue, but to Jerry, it stung. The shower drain let out a throaty gargle as the squeak of the shower head signaled the expected return of a freshly cleansed yet most likely still percolating Joyce. Jerry rushed into the kitchen in stocking feet and began to plate the remaining sections of the cake. The odd bits went into the trash and the cake plate was promptly cleaned and dried. He started the coffee maker and readied the two cups with milk and two sugar cubes for Joyce. He turned the lights to the lowest setting, switched on the radio, and placed the plated cake on each side table next to each parlor chair.

Joyce emerged in her house dress. Her hair was down, one side pinned up behind the ear, a sweeping golden blonde that made Jerry weak when she wore it like that. Her bedroom hair. She never wore it around anyone else, mind you. He shivered just looking at her.

'And what is this?' She asked lowly.

'I thought we'd take it easy for a while, stay up and listen to the radio.'

'Hmm.' Joyce eyed the hunks of cake on each table. With all the salt she could muster she sighed and said, 'Well, I suppose we should try to enjoy what's left of that misery.'

Jerry relaxed a bit, but not by much. Agreeability this soon after a debacle usually spelled covert trouble later. But he wanted to go with it, he might even attempt to nuzzle her this evening. Hopefully, they'd end the program with a Gershwin tune before the signal signed off.

'Ladies and gentlemen, the director of the Mercury Theatre and star of these broadcasts, Orson Welles,' the radio boomed.

'Oh! I really like him. So handsome.' Joyce smirked into her coffee. She sipped lightly and looked at Jerry plainly. 'Perfect.'

Jerry smiled as the broadcast went on.

'We know now that in the early years of the twentieth century, this world was being watched closely by an intelligence greater than man's, and yet as mortal. We know now that as human beings busied themselves about their various concerns they were scrutinized and studied, perhaps almost as narrowly as a man with a microscope might scrutinize the transient creatures that swarm and multiply in a drop of water. With infinite complacency, people went to and fro over the earth—'.

Orson Welles trailed off as Joyce interrupted. Jerry fidgeted; he was getting interested.

'Do you agree with that?' Joyce asked.

'With what?'

'That we're being watched, like zoo animals? I would think we'd all be very awkward to watch.' Joyce scooped a piece of cake into her mouth and chewed slowly. Methodically.

'This is lovely,' she said. 'Shame there isn't more.'

Jerry sighed and threw out the thought of nuzzling altogether. There was no letting this cake business go tonight or tomorrow. Perhaps by the weekend if he was lucky. There'd be no listening for DiMaggio's moves this week. She'd see to that.

'In the thirty-ninth year of the twentieth century came the great disillusionment. It was near the end of October. Business was better. The war scare was over. More men were back at work. Sales were picking up.' Orson continued, as did Joyce.

Jerry was getting annoyed. Usually, they quietly enjoyed a program or two together and conferred after the fact but tonight Joyce had other plans to drag the knife across Jerry's chest a little longer.

'I think they need to be talking about the women who single-handedly supported the men while they were at war. This country could've dissolved altogether, you know. And now you put us back in front of machines to keep another war going. Pity.'

'Maybe send you over there. I suppose you'd get it in shape in no time.' Jerry scraped across his plate with the edge of his fork, causing Joyce to shudder, and continued enjoying his cake. Joyce began to speak and stopped short.

'With a touch of the Spanish, Ramón Raquello leads off with 'La Cumparsita.'"

'Tango? On a Sunday night? What are they after?' She mashed the last bits of cake against her fork and sucked on the end. 'I hope we don't get bombarded with children tomorrow night. Fifteen is about all I can stand.'

'We never get more than ten and you know it. Now just pipe down and enjoy the music.' He could feel her glare bore a hole clean through his face and made the choice to ignore it and slowly hum along to a tune he didn't know. At least one of them would enjoy it.

'Ladies and gentlemen, we interrupt our program of dance music to bring you a special bulletin from the Intercontinental Radio News. At twenty minutes before eight, central time, Professor Farrell of the Mount Jennings Observatory, Chicago, Illinois, reports observing several explosions of incandescent gas, occurring at regular intervals on the planet Mars. The spectroscope indicates the gas to be hydrogen and moving towards the earth with enormous velocity. Professor Pierson of the Observatory at Princeton confirms Farrell's observation and describes the phenomenon as, quote, 'like a jet of blue flame shot from a gun,' unquote. We now return you to the music of Ramón Raquello, playing for you in the Meridian Room of the Park Plaza Hotel, situated in downtown New York.'

Joyce's brow furrowed. She slowly set the plate on the side table and rose in melancholy.

'More coffee?'

Jerry waved her on. He nestled into the chair and crossed his arms over his chest. The night already had a chill to end a thousand marriages but the stillness of the outdoors, the coldness of the indoors, and now the errant phenomenon created a recipe of distemper in Jerry.

Something in his belly stirred and warmed and coiled its way to his chest, then neck, and caused a lightening hot flame in his cheeks. His mouth opened and the sudden temperature change caught the words.

'Why do you have to be such a bitch?' A chair squeaked against the kitchen floor. Silence. For the longest while. Silence. At this point in the game, Jerry would wither, wait for the clipped sentences and snotty demeanor but tonight he was chasing fire. Jerry stood and pounded into the kitchen to a calm Joyce pouring hot coffee into her cup.

'I said, Joyce, why do you always have to be such a bitch?'

'You would think someone who'd ruined an evening would have a milder temper.'

Jerry stepped into the kitchen further, making Joyce stiffen.

'You would think someone with all the warmth of a deli fish could stop acting like she got shot in the guts every time I had a grievance. At least I can say what I'm angry about.'

'What exactly is your problem, dear?'

Jerry bolted out of the room and blared the radio, sending Joyce flying in.

'Are you crazy? The neighbors!'

'Fuck 'em! Let them hear this or the sound of you standing on my last nerve.'

An announcer broke through the last remnants of Tango.

'Now, nearer home comes a special bulletin from Trenton, New Jersey. It is reported that at 8:50 P.M. a huge, flaming object, believed to be a meteorite, fell on a farm in the neighborhood of Grovers Mill, New Jersey, twenty-two miles from Trenton. The flash in the sky was visible within a radius of several hundred miles and the noise of the impact was heard as far north as Elizabeth. We have dispatched a special mobile unit to the scene and will have our commentator, Carl Phillips, give you a word picture of the scene as soon as he can reach there from Princeton.'

Joyce gasped. 'I hope no one was hurt!'

'Maybe it's the firing squad coming for you, ya harpy.'

'Too bad you didn't choke on your cake, Jerry. Wouldn't be the last thing you scarfed down this month.'

Jerry scowled and stood. 'What did you just say?'

Joyce began to cry. Jerry softened but stiffened again. The first real trickle of human emotion in years from his wife and he couldn't capture it in the ways he wanted to. No tenderness, no 'there, there.' Just the white-hot heat of disdain.

'Everyone asks about it. Your weight. Christ, Jerry you were a footballer in college, a tough, rugged player. My big, broad hero. Now you're all jelly and depression. Why bother to look good for something you can't even look at? Haven't bought a new dress in years, what's the point? I can't bring myself to even act excited.'

'Is this about the cake?'

'Oh God dammit, Jerry!'

A quick static and hurried voice cut between them.

'Hundreds of cars are parked in a field in back of us and the police are trying to rope off the roadway leading into the farm but it's no use. They're breaking right through. Cars' headlights throw an enormous spotlight on the pit where the object's half buried. Now some of the more daring souls are venturing near the edge. Their silhouettes stand out against the metal sheen.'

'What the hell?' Jerry walked closer to the radio and turned down the volume. He stood with his hand on the top, half expecting it to blow open or shut down. At most, get back to the music. The soundtrack to the dissolution of his marriage.

The men on the radio continued. Warbled conversations, many from far away, a slight panic in all their voices. Jerry and Joyce took knowingly worried glances at each other. He closed his eyes and sighed.

'Would you like to leave me?'

Joyce sat heavily in the armchair. 'I don't know what I want. I dream every day of getting away. Traveling west to see my sister and never coming back. Starting over, coloring my hair. Dressing more colorfully, things like that.'

'Anything else?'

The voices on the radio were tense now. The couple's attention again diverted. On a knife's edge, eagerly awaiting the final boom to lower between them and wondering what the hell else was happening in the world. In New Jersey. So close to home.

'I don't know what to think. The metal casing is definitely extraterrestrial . . . not found on this earth. Friction with the earth's atmosphere usually tears holes in a meteorite. This thing is smooth and, as you can see, of cylindrical shape. Just a minute! Something's happening! Ladies and gentlemen, this is terrific! This end of the thing is beginning to flake off! The top is beginning to rotate like a screw and the thing must be hollow! She's movin'! Look, the darn thing's unscrewing! Stand back, there! Keep those men back, I tell you! Maybe there's men in it trying to escape! It's red hot, they'll burn to a cinder! Keep back there. Keep those idiots back!'

Joyce took a leaping step towards the radio and brushed against Jerry.

'Jesus Christ, Jerry! Extraterrestrial? Like Spacemen?'

'Impossible!'

The couple stared into the radio like children pressed against a nickelodeon. The men on the radio went on about the metal spacecraft and its furious shaking and, eventually, its inhabitants.

'Good heavens, something's wriggling out of the shadow like a gray snake. Now it's another one, and another one, and another one! They look like tentacles to me. I can see the thing's body now. It's large, large as a bear and it glistens like wet leather. But that face, ladies and gentlemen, it's indescribable. I can hardly force myself to keep looking at it, so awful. The eyes are black and gleam like a serpent. The mouth is V-shaped with saliva dripping from its rimless lips that seem to quiver and pulsate. The monster or whatever it is can hardly move. It seems weighed down.'

Joyce clutched at her house coat and began to sob.

'Dear God, they're coming!'

A pound at their door pulled screams out of them both. Jerry ran to the door with Joyce close behind him. Another bang. Jerry flung open the door to Sam Ghenderson's panicked face.

'Are you leaving?'

'Leaving where?' Jerry felt Joyce clutching at the back of his shirt.

'Leaving town! We're heading upstate, you're welcome to follow us. We just wanted to let you know we're leaving as soon as possible!' Sam was sweating on his shirt, a V-shaped pattern of panic and hurry.

'Why are you leaving?' Joyce's voice was at least a half octave higher than usual.

'Didn't you hear? Aren't you listening? Aliens! We're being invaded!' Sam wiped his brow in frustration and turned to hear his wife scream from their open kitchen window. Dixie Ghenderson's panic cut through the exchange like a hot wire.

'They've just attacked! Oh Sam, hurry!'

'I'm sorry you two. But if you're not leaving now, I—I'm just sorry.' Sam ran down their path and hopped over the adjoining hedge. Dark child-height shadows pedaled in front of an aging body being dragged along by Dixie. The car looked packed as it reversed heavily and leaned slightly as it squealed out of sight. Jerry waved and felt the stupidity of it instantly. Four more cars sped down the street. Lights began to go out in the windows of houses. Darkness came as Jerry and Joyce stood in the only lit beacon on 11th Avenue.

They walked slowly back to the panicked voices and clutter-filled bellows of the broadcast. There would be no more Tangos. No Gershwin, or Ramón Raquello. Just calamity and fear, and anger and sadness. And death.

The announcer's voice was dire.

'Incredible as it may seem, both the observations of science and the evidence of our eyes lead to the inescapable assumption that those strange beings who landed in the Jersey farmlands tonight are the vanguard of an invading army from the planet Mars. The battle which took place tonight at Grovers Mill has ended in one of the most startling defeats ever suffered by an army in modern times; seven thousand men armed with rifles and machine guns pitted against a single Martian fighting machine. One hundred and twenty known survivors. The rest strewn over the battle area from Grovers Mill to Plainsboro, crushed, and trampled to death under the metal feet of the monster, or burned to cinders by its heat ray. The monster is now in control of the middle section of New Jersey and has effectively cut the state through its center. Communication lines are down from Pennsylvania to the Atlantic Ocean.'

'So, this is it? This is how it ends? Fight off Austrians just to die here in my own living room? What a kick in the pants.'

Joyce wrung her hands and stomped her feet lightly into the carpet. Panic was taking over. Jerry turned to her and watched her mechanically go through the stages of it. The deep inhales and exhalations, the rise and fall of her shoulders, the gasps of breath that quickened and never slowed.

My God, she's going to pass out, he thought.

He made no move towards her. Let her. Let her gasp out, eyes wide like the dead fish she is. Her eyes traveled to the motionless man, clinging to the radio. She took a deep breath and leaned back into the armchair; small pants gave way to longer, deeper breaths.

'Are you finished?'

'God damn you, Jerry.'

'Was there anything else?'

'Anything else about what, Jerry?'

'Other than the fact that it's taken me twenty years to put on sixty pounds, the fact that everyone talks about me, that you don't feel attractive, that I'm a nuisance, un-neighborly. Was there anything else?'

Joyce leaned forward, her breath regulating. She began to cry silently. 'Yes.'

'And that is?'

'I think about killing you every day.'

A flurry of fuzzed voices mixed with metal shot through the radio, vibrating Jerry's hand.

' . . . I'm speaking from the roof of the Broadcasting Building, New York City. The bells you hear are ringing to warn the people to evacuate the city as the Martians approach. Estimated in the last two hours, three million people have moved out along the roads to the north . . . Hutchison River Parkway still kept open for motor traffic. Avoid bridges to Long Island . . . hopelessly jammed. All communication with Jersey Shore closed ten minutes ago. No more defenses. Our army is . . . wiped out . . . artillery, air force, everything wiped out. This may be the last broadcast. We'll stay here to the end...'

Jerry lowered the volume.

'What are you doing?!' cried Joyce.

'Letting it be. Either you kill me, or they do. Nothing else to be excited about I suppose.'

'I—I suppose.'

Jerry sat in his armchair as the last of the cars buzzed by. They were all alone on 11th Avenue. Left to fend for themselves in a war already brewing inside four walls and a picture window. Amongst the lace curtains handed down from Joyce's mother. Along the lowboy carried over from Ireland by his grandfather and great-uncle. Above the marigold carpet that Joyce had her heart set on in New York, in 1916.

'What is your favorite way to kill me?' Jerry asked, looking out the picture window at the navy, starless sky.

'Jerry!' Joyce pulled both hands to her mouth and sobbed again.

'I mean. What is your most often thought-about way to take out old Jerry?

Joyce couldn't form a word. Her tears clutched her throat like a valve fastened tightly on a faucet.

'Joyce?' Jerry's eyes began to well.

There'd been tension on and on for the last decade. Not as rich as her old friends and not as happy as her new ones. Jerry had gotten passed over for a position on a banking route due to lack of stamina, as they so kindly put it. Joyce never grew out of that embarrassment's shadow. And that's when it dawned on him.

No one was talking about him, no one probably cared about it for that matter. And that's what irked Joyce the most. They weren't the Smiths or the Joneses or the goddamn Ghendersons with their manicured lawns and loving extended family and their fair-haired, close-in-age boy and girl children.

Children. Too expensive. Too much on Joyce. The freedom of heading on all the promised trips they planned but never went on. Jerry Boyd would have done anything for the sweetest, most beautiful woman he'd ever known, but he didn't.

'Joyce?'

'Jerry, don't make me do this. I was angry, I didn't mean it. Let's just wait for the police or the army or something to tell us where to go.'

'I don't think much of anyone is coming, Joyce. Just you and me, until it isn't. Now. Tell me how.'

Joyce stood as if entranced, her features softened. She glanced at the radio and closed her eyes. Realizing that Jerry was right. It was just the two of them. The announcer continued.

'I keep watch at the window. From time to time, I catch sight of a . . . Martian above the black smoke. The smoke still holds the house in its black coil, but . . . at length there is a hissing sound and suddenly I see a Martian mounted on his machine, spraying the air with a jet of steam, as if to dissipate the smoke. I watch in a corner as his huge metal legs nearly brush against the house.'

A strange man's voice, separate from the announcers. 'They're taking witness accounts now. It's all coming to an end.'

She thought. Her voice was weak, fearful.

'You, well, you'd be sitting in that chair.' Joyce faced the picture window and closed the lace curtains and then the heavy curtains. 'And I'd make some coffee.'

'Mhhmm.' Jerry watched her breathlessly, half dreamy romance, half floating above, watching his death sentence.

'Please don't make me go on.'

'Joyce. It's my dying wish.'

Joyce recoiled. 'And then I'd put the herbicide from the garden in your coffee. Then I'd sit and watch you.'

'Poison. I wouldn't figure. Go on.'

Jerry half listened to a long account of Martian meetings through the radio waves. This odd calm of impending death gave him an interesting perspective. Youth makes you wish for such grandiose things that nothing seems attainable enough. It's the insignificant things you forget to do or consciously stop doing because something will always matter more. House payments, groceries. Hot water. Rides in the country fade away. Long trips to Upstate New York get penciled in the twelfth of never. Babies get their lack of fruition justified by petty bills and grievances.

Funny, isn't it, he thought, *Ghenderson's never going to get to use the RM-80 anyway.*

Joyce began again, pulling him out of his stupor. 'And when it had finished you, I'd put on my cleaning gloves and slit your throat with the letter opener. No chance of breathing again even if they could help you.'

Jerry stared at her feigning defiance. He'd brought her here. She very well could've been trying to get his goat with such heinous words, but he'd never know now. He'd pushed her too far.

'And then what would you do?'

Joyce walked over to him and knelt by his armchair.

'I would finish your coffee.'

Jerry's hand clasped hard over hers and pulled her in, kissing her passionately. Joyce matched his pressure. What excitement was this? How horrifying a scenario of calculated murder and alien invasion, wet ends of hair, and poisonous coffee.

'Then let's do that.'

'Jerry?' Joyce stood quickly. 'You're crazy! Jerry, no!'

'What choice do we have? Die a slow alien death? Or go gently, in our home?'

'Oh God! What will everyone say?'

'There is no everyone, Joyce. We're possibly the last two people in the state of New Jersey. What do you say?'

The stranger came crawling back through the airwaves.

'They got themselves in solid; they wrecked the greatest country in the world. Those green stars, they're probably falling somewhere every night. They've only lost one machine. There isn't anything to do. We're done. We're licked.'

'See what I mean?'

Joyce looked at him endearingly and laid a kiss on his forehead. 'More coffee, Jerry?'

'Yes, please. No letter-opener this time.'

Joyce winked and began to heat the percolator one last time. She headed to the porch bin to retrieve the weed killer and placed a delicately measured teaspoon in each cup. Jerry padded his slacks and stood, teary-eyed. He took stock of their photos and mementos, of odd furniture that didn't fit, of silly knickknacks Joyce collected from town fairs. A story attached to each one. Joyce followed in with two steaming cups. A salted coffee scent filled the living room.

'Here.' Jerry struggled to sit cross-legged in front of the radio. 'Join me.'

Joyce sat closely at his side and put her head on his shoulder.

'I'm sorry about the cake, Joyce. I'm sorry for everything I promised and never gave you. I do love you so much.'

'And I love you, and I'm sorry for never saying how I feel and letting it build up. I don't think I could go on without you.' Joyce sniffled. 'I'm glad we're doing this together.'

'Best trip idea you've had.' Jerry kissed her forehead and listened to the broadcast. The screams had ceased, and the crunch of destruction and desperation was meandering through the voices now. Jerry and Joyce were on their way to a vacation spot of their choice. A toast with dandelion wine to the good days and choices made.

The Boyd's clinked their cups together and downed their coffee in one gulp. Wide-eyed, they waited. Feverishly, Jerry began to sweat, and Joyce lurched and turned purple. Jerry's mouth frothed as he fell to his side gripping at Joyce's house coat. The veins in Joyce's face burst from the skin as a thick sludge of vomit burnt into the carpet. Jerry twitched repeatedly, never losing his hold on Joyce, who rolled on her side to face him. Face to face in a crooked, painful nuzzle. Finally.

The broadcast clicked on for a few minutes as a familiar voice re-emerged.

'This is Orson Welles, ladies, and gentlemen, out of character to assure you that 'The War of The Worlds' has no further significance than as the holiday offering it was intended to be. The Mercury Theatre's own radio version of dressing up in a sheet, jumping out of a bush, and saying Boo! Starting now, we couldn't soap all your windows and steal all your garden gates by tomorrow night . . . so we did the next best thing. We annihilated the world before your very ears, and utterly destroyed the C.B.S. You will be relieved, I hope, to learn that we didn't mean it and that both institutions are still open for business. So, goodbye everybody, and remember please, for the next day or so, the terrible lesson you learned tonight. That grinning, glowing, globular invader of your living room is an inhabitant of the pumpkin patch, and if your doorbell rings and nobody's there, that was no Martian . . . it's Halloween.'

Daylight cracked through the bottom of the curtain seams. Birds chirped and sang. A car roared up the road and footsteps raced up the pathway to 21 11th Avenue. A series of raps gave way to a click of a doorknob.

It was said that you could hear Sam Ghenderson's scream a mile away.

***This story contains excerpts from the 1938 Columbia Broadcasting System's Radio Broadcast of* The War of the Worlds, *read by Orson Welles and the Mercury Theatre on the Air, now in the public domain.*

THE TOWER

STAINED GLASS

"GRETEL SHOOK OUT her apron, scattering pearls and precious stones around the room, and Hansel added to them by throwing one handful after the other from his pockets. Now all their cares were at an end, and they lived happily together." Pete sighed. His breath sent white tendrils into the air.

He closed the storybook and patted his daughter's leg, catching a glimpse of his hand's shadow in the candle glow. He made a crude shadow rabbit head running towards her. Christine giggled loudly. A deep guttural groan split their happiness wide open. Pete's hands fumbled to her face, covering her mouth tightly.

"Under the covers, now!"

Pete's eyes were wild, darting around all the corners of the room. Moving from his daughter's bedside to the candle near the busy colored stained-glass window, he quickly blew it out, sending the room into shadow.

From beneath the comforter, she shivered excitedly, "The Creakers!"

"That's right. Now we have to trick them." His voice was low, metered as he tread lightly to the small dresser, extinguishing another candle. Pete crouched down next to the bed. "Shh, Christine!"

"Sorry, Daddy," she whispered.

The groans gave way to screeches and howls, pants, and taps against the glass. Christine tried to stifle her giggles but instead inhaled sharply and exhaled in a cackle. Pete hit against the bed, stiffly, bringing all movement and noise within the room to a stop. He bit his lower lip, his teeth slipping from the sweat that had trickled into it. He pawed around the room towards the doorway. Moving left to the hallway desk, his fingers found the ham radio. He slowly pulled the headphone cushion to a small transceiver. A tape recorder clicked on, spilling muffled animal sounds into the night and sending the otherworldly treading away from the lake house.

Christine pulled her messy-haired head out from beneath the covers.

"Daddy?" she whispered.

Pete slowly made his way back into her bedroom.

"Can we talk now?"

Pete sighed. "Yes, yes, honey. We can talk now."

"Why do the Creakers keep coming?" She struggled to sit upright and leaned on her side.

"Probably because they're hungry. So, they roam like any animal, searching. Like the polar bears."

"But there's more Creakers than polar bears, Daddy."

Pete's breath was quick and shallow, and he wrung his hands in the darkness. "What makes you say that?" He settled back down onto the bed.

"There just sounds like there's a lot of 'em. Can you tell me about them again?"

"Why don't you start it this time?" Pete sidled to the wall, his feet dangling off the edge of the bed.

Christine darted up. "So, once upon a time, there were these animals called Hummelsplapiens-."

Pete laughs. "Homosapiens."

"Homosapiens, right." Christine continued. "And they touched something that made them really sick and then some died off but then the rest are still hungry? Is that right?"

"Almost."

"Well, that's why I wanted you to tell it. I always mess it up!" Christine flops onto her back.

"Alright, alright." Pete shifted to lean into Christine. "These Homosapiens were exposed to something called an agitator. It disrupted the way their body should work, so to survive, their bodies had to turn into something else. Something—." He knew what he wanted to say, but it wouldn't leave his throat. Not now. Perhaps not ever.

"So, they just roam around trying to figure out how to live again and eat and sleep and travel. It's all very hard for them." Pete crossed his arms and let his body collapse along the wall.

"Why can't we just tell them where to go?"

"No!" Pete corrected. "No, we can't do that. They have to learn for themselves."

"They sound so silly."

"They do, don't they? Now, you should get some sleep."

Christine sighed, exasperated. "Okay."

"I'll be right across the hall." Pete leaned in to kiss her on the forehead.

"What if they come back?" She whispered.

"They won't tonight, I promise." Pete pushed to the edge of the bed and stood. "And no lighting that candle again 'til tomorrow after supper, okay?"

"Yes, Daddy." Christine reluctantly rolled over.

Pete watched her for a moment, still thinking of that forbidden word in the darkness and watching the grey-black beyond the blue, cream, and purple stained glass. He backed out of the room and eyed the front door. A door festooned with several styles of drapes hanging from a single rod, that sagged under the weight of the various fabrics. Six clicks of various locks and he slowly turned the knob to the front door, stepping onto the small, enclosed porch. The walls were thickly boarded over with differing planks and slats of wood and metal, fronted by stacked furniture. The small room was a wicked black, save for a small relay of light through a hole in a knotty pine. Pete leveled his eye at it and recoiled. He took a deep inhale and returned his gaze.

A tall figure loomed singularly near the porch, facing away from him. It swayed, meandering through the front yard. A desolate place of ash and cinder. Of brown char and orange sky. The being turned quickly in Pete's direction, but Pete made no sudden moves, no gasps, no rustle. Its head was mangled, open, seemingly sliced in half yet not removed. Its unharmed eye searched the air for something unknown. Its skin was grey. Shockingly cold against the beaming pink of its muscle. It drooled heavily and, dismayed by the empty search, turned away from the house as if pulled. Its bones and muscles jerked, causing its movements to jar, halt, and fire all at once, a putrid pigeon walk into the night. Pete stepped slowly back out of the porch, focused on the small hole. He entered the hallway and gently closed the door. He painstakingly locked the locks and headed to his room, across the hall from an already sleeping Christine.

Christine blinked furiously at the gleam piercing through a small skylight in her ceiling. Three skylights were blackened. *Tarnished,* her father would say when she asked. She sat upright quickly, eyeing the top of the small dresser. Ham, cold.

"Aw come on! Daddy, you didn't wake me up!" Christine popped out into the hallway. "Daddy?" She padded lightly into his makeshift bedroom. "Daddy?"

She traveled to a small side table where a thick copy of *Jack and the Beanstalk and Other Stories* sat. She smirked and picked up a thin piece of paper.

Out getting snacks for story time!—Dad

She lingered at the small bookshelf stationed next to the shuttered window and thumbed at the newspaper mache'd to the window behind. She pulled at it, cracking the paper and slicing a tiny cut on her finger.

"Ouch!" She put her finger in her mouth and sucked as she took stock of the tall stack of newspapers. She pulled the top paper, pulling apart its yellowing pages carefully with one hand. She laid it gently on the large sofa bed and turned her head to the right to read its fading headlines.

NO STOP TO CONTAGION IN SIGHT. CDC BAFFLED BY BIO-CHEMICAL VASCULAR NECROSIS SWEEPING THE U.S.

A thud in the hallway shook her. She unconsciously pulled the paper at both ends, sending a tear down the middle.

"Oh no!" she whispered. She hurriedly refolded the newspaper and placed it hard on the stack, making it lean and scattering the entire stack to the floor. Another thud had her racing out of the room.

"Daddy?" she shouted. "Um, I was just looking for something else to read before story time."

A grunt echoed in the kitchen. Its gurgling noise sent Christine flinging toward the wall as she edged slowly toward the sound.

A short being in a floral sack paced the kitchen. Its movements didn't complement its legs, which were raw to the bone, flesh-free. Its split head spilled forth in a bulbous jumble of sores. It turned to Christine and grunted heavily. Christine screamed and the being lurched forward, arms outstretched, its upper body moving independently of its bottom. Christine ran alongside the kitchen wall to the basement door and began to run down the stairs. The being followed her steadily, making Christine duck on the third step in fear. A wisp of foul-smelling floral fabric grazed Christine's left cheek as the being fell over her, tumbling down the cement steps, its neck catching on the railing as its body continued to the basement floor.

Christine watched the mess of floral print and blood, its gaping neck gurgling heavily. She raced up the stairs, slamming the basement door shut and backing away. She shoved a kitchen chair under the doorknob. She'd seen her father do that once.

"Christine!" Pete shouted, spinning her around. She lunged at him, in full cry.

"Daddy, it got in!" Christine pressed her wet face into Pete's blood-stained chest.

"What, baby, what got in?" Pete held her tightly.

"A Creaker."

Pete knelt and grasped her face tightly. "Where? Where is it?"

"It's in the basement. I think . . . ," barely catching her breath, "I think it's dead."

Pete patted Christine on the legs and arms, he checked her neck and cheeks. "It didn't hurt you, did it?"

"No. Just chased me. Daddy, don't let them in!" Christine's breath was quick and panicked. She wheezed, tears staining her now brightly red cheeks.

"I won't . . . ," he stopped, turning to look at the mess of newspapers in his bedroom. He turned back to her, wide-eyed. "Christine, what happened here?"

"I—I—was l-looking—"

"Christine, breathe."

She took a ragged inhale. "I was looking for something else to read before story time."

Pete swallowed hard. "Did you read them?"

"Only a few things. I didn't mean to knock 'em all over, honest." Christine's eyes welled up again. Pete patted her on the head and took her hand.

"I'm going to clean them up. Stand here." He squared Christine's shoulders against the doorframe of the makeshift bedroom. Christine took stock of her father. He was bloodstained, dirty, bruised. His pants were wet.

"Daddy?"

"Yeah?"

"You okay?"

Pete groaned as he leaned to pick up the newspapers.

"Yeah, baby, I'm okay, just tired." He placed his hand gently on a weeping wound in his hip. He pushed the papers lightly together in a pile with his foot.

AIRBORNE NECROTIC FEVER SWEEPS ACROSS THE EASTERN SEABOARD

Catching a glimpse of the New York Times, he stared wearily at a large picture of college students being escorted out of UConn by men in hazmat suits.

ARE FOREIGN STUDENTS TO BLAME FOR THE WIDESPREAD CONTAMINATION? PRESIDENT OLIVER IS WAITING FOR AN ANSWER.

He brushed another paper aside,

"CLOSE BORDERS NOW!" DEMANDS SPEAKER OF THE HOUSE.

On another front page, a crowd of people being set ablaze are met with people in yellow riot gear. One face in the frame, directly into the camera, in agony.

"A MELTING POT NO MORE. CONTAINMENT AND REMOVAL CONTINUE AS NECROTIC FEVER WAGES ON."

He knelt, putting his body between Christine and the papers. He spread them out lightly. More of the same but one, one so very different. And so much closer to the truth.

The People's Messenger, a local community college outpost of past journalism students.

LOCAL CHILD SUSPECTED IN WIDESPREAD CONTAMINATION

New Hampshire—Meredith Elementary School 1st Grader Christine Bellamy is a person of interest in the fast-spreading virus within the Tri-State area. Bellamy fell ill in class last Thursday morning and was sent to the health office, where she vomited. It's said all staff became violently ill immediately and Christine left school with a parent. Bellamy has not been seen nor has there been any contact with her parents. The school staff became ill in the following days and Meredith Elementary has yet to reopen. The CDC and the Federal Government have yet to send out a bulletin on eight-year-old Christine and her family even after the tip, but we ask that citizens contact these agencies should they

encounter them. Citizens are warned not to
engage, as the child is deemed highly
infectious.

Pete's hands shook trying to pull the papers back into a pile.
His mouth was dry, face pallid. He stared into the distance in
panic. Closing his eyes, he let it find him. The scent of lilacs.

"I don't know where it started honey, they just said she wasn't
feeling well, they called me to come get her." Pete shuffled in a
waddling Christine. Her face was pale.

"Come on tiger, into bed."

"Daddy, I'm tired." She climbed in and rolled away from him.

"I know baby. Mom's gonna make you some soup and then I
want you to rest, okay?"

She grunted and tucked her face into the pillow. Pete closed
the door slightly.

"Babe?" A small voice whispered. Beth, all five foot two against
his six feet five in the hallway. "We're out of soup."

"Damn. Alright. I'll head out. She looks like she's gonna sleep
this off." Pete ran his hands along her waist and kissed her on the
forehead. "Anything else while I'm out?"

"Cherry Garcia?" Beth's eyes lit up.

"Again?"

Beth grimaced.

"Got it. Be back in a bit." Pete grabbed his keys off the rack and
headed out the door. He swiveled around.

"What are you wearing?"

Beth smiled. "You like it? Eau du Lilac something or other. It's
from a magazine."

"I'll pick that up too." He smiled.

"Yeah good luck, I don't think they sell that at Wegmans."

Muzak swam in the air of the Wegmans parking lot as Pete
stuffed two brown paper shopping bags in the trunk. He was
startled by a man vomiting beside his car.

"Sir, you alright?" He walked slowly towards the man as another man ran past him, almost knocking him down. "Jesus, man!"

"You better get outta here, everyone's getting sick inside. Gas leak I think, the place might blow!"

Pete slammed down the trunk and rushed into the car. Turning the ignition, he spotted a stout woman in a floral-patterned dress. Christine's art teacher, Ms. Best. She lurched and projectile vomited against her car. Pete peeled out of the parking lot. He weaved through the traffic of abandoned and stopped vehicles.

Cracking open the kitchen entrance from the garage he stumbled, "Beth!" Silence. "Beth!"

"Daddy?" Christine stood in the hallway outside her room.

Pete rushed to her side. "Baby? You okay?"

Christine shook her head furiously. "Mommy's not getting up." She pointed into her bedroom. Beth's body twitched angrily. A pool of bloody vomit enshrined her convulsing head. She staggered to her knees and turned swiftly to the door, her skin stretched, still attached to the rank pool on the carpet. Beth lunged toward the door. Pete pulled it shut, panicked.

Beth pounded frantically from the other side. A screeching sound blended with guttural grunts. A blunt force slam breaks into the door, jostling the frame. Pete quickly grabbed a dining room chair and jutted it under the doorknob. The door rocked wildly as the sounds continued.

"What's wrong with mommy?" Christine screamed.

"Baby, come on. Mommy's sick and we have to go get her help. Come here!"

Christine ran past Pete and held onto him in full sob. "Daddy!"

"Come on, let—" A large crack broke his gaze on Christine. "Go take a bag from the kitchen closet, you know the big ones that mommy takes to the store?"

Christine nodded quickly.

"Take all of your clothes out of the laundry and put them in that bag and I'll meet you downstairs."

"But Daddy!"

"Now, Christine!"

Pete began to sob. He reached over to Christine for another large shopping bag. He piled food from the pantry into the bag.

"Baby, can you take this and your clothes and meet me in the garage?"

"No, I wanna stay with you!"

"The garage, baby. I'll be right there."

Christine fearfully took the kitchen steps down to the garage. Pete took another bag from the closet and headed back down the hallway. Grunts and pants echoed into the narrow space. At the end of the hall lay the rose-patterned bedspread Beth saw on Pinterest that he surprised her with on her birthday. Pete ambled against the wall towards their bedroom. He entered the bedroom and rushed to the closet, emptying his hangers of clothes, emptying his dresser drawers. A bang against the door again made him gasp. He ran back down the hallway.

"Daddy?"

He eyed Christine's bedroom door. No grunts or pants.

Christine stood in the doorway of the kitchen. Pete put his finger to his lips and motioned for her to go back to the garage.

Christine shook her head no. "There's a lady out there," she whispered.

Pete rushed past Christine's room as Beth burst through the door, knocking him down.

"Run, Christine!"

Beth was crazed, her eyes red, and what was left of her mouth was foaming. Pete wriggled to a stand. Beth's shoulders and hips pointed in two different directions, but she pounced towards Pete, missing him. Pete and Christine bounded down the steps to the garage and slammed the door. He knocked over a filing cabinet, blocking the exit. Pete threw the bags into the back seat.

"Get in the car!"

Christine hurriedly stepped in. Pete's eyes widened. A small crowd had gathered in the street. Pale, meandering.

Pete quickly entered the car. "I want you to cover your eyes."

"Why Daddy?"

"Cover your eyes, baby, please," he sobbed.

Pete opened the garage door, drawing the attention of the serpentine crowd.

"Come on, come on!" With the garage door in clearance, Pete gunned it in reverse into the street. Christine screamed.

"Keep 'em covered, okay?" Pete spun the car into drive and

slalomed through the now-angry crowd. Some gave chase on broken legs, some panted and squawked. Beth's jagged body tumbled into the street and stared.

Christine weepily asked, "Where are we going, Daddy?"

"We're gonna go to the lake house for a bit, okay? Just 'til you're feeling better."

"What's wrong with Mommy?"

"I don't know, baby, I don't know."

"Can I open my eyes now?"

"Not for a while yet. I'll let you know." Pete broke down and pushed his foot harder onto the gas.

"Daddy?"

Pete shook heavily, his hip stiff, his chest rising and falling frantically. His eyes traveled around the room. The yellow newspapers at the corner of his eyes pulled him back to center.

"Daddy!"

Pete spun, almost falling into a shaking Christine.

"The Creakers are here!"

Cracks and groans flooded the home. Screeches and pants, clicks and howls, stomps and slick foot patter enveloped the hallway. He rushed to Christine.

"Baby, get back!" Christine stayed behind Pete.

Pete pushed backward on Christine, heading slowly towards the front door as the group of Creakers snaked into the hallway. Their pace was slow and calculated. On uneven limbs, they seemed to be in a time step. Pete unlocked the front door and pushed Christine into the small porch, slamming the door behind him. The grunts and screeches peaked. Pete covered his ears and knelt, pulling Christine close.

"Baby, I want you to listen very closely to me. We're gonna go out this door and we're gonna run to the little boat by the dock. Do you remember the boat?" Pete began to pull the motley panels of wood off with his bare hands, unearthing the front door.

"Why are they here?" Christine heaved, her breath ragged.

"You said they were like polar bears and they're not! They're monsters and you didn't tell me!"

"Christine, listen!"

Christine pushed him away. "No! Why are they here? You said we were safe, you said they wouldn't come back!"

Pete sobbed. "I know baby, I'm so sorry, but we have to go now."

Christine threw punches at Pete's stomach. "You promised! I don't wanna go on the boat. I wanna stay here. I want Mommy. I wanna stay here!"

Pete picked her up, burying his face in her hair. "I'm so sorry baby, we're going now." He turned the locks on the front door and pushed it open. Christine kicked and bucked her body back, screaming. The grunts gave way to a collective high-pitched howl surrounding them. The front yard was full of broken inhuman dolls with broken limbs, melted faces, and bloated, pale bodies.

"Christ," he whispered.

Christine wriggled free and stepped down. She turned, eyes wide. Pete grabbed her and held her close to him.

"Daddy?" Christine's voice was thin.

"Yes, baby?" Pete was weary, locked in the gaze of a hundred Creakers ambling slowly across the property.

"You didn't get sick."

"What, baby?"

"You didn't get sick. Mommy got sick. Nothing happened to us."

"I know baby, I tried to get us away from everything."

"Are we going to get sick now?"

Pete held her tight and kissed the top of her head. Christine was stoic. She stepped forward and Pete scrambled, tripping on the last step onto his wounded hip. She was four large steps out of his reach before he could stand.

"Christine!"

"Daddy?"

"Christine! Come here!"

"Daddy, look at them."

Pete surveyed the front property. The Creakers had slowed. Some had stopped and fallen to what was left of their knees. One by one they all fell down. Knees on earth, limbs outstretched.

"What are they doing?" Christine stepped further forward. Pete did not follow. Something within him was planted to the ground, taking root. He watched Christine meander through the broken bodies. Not one movement from the monsters, not a quiver, just a longing gaze from their festering eyes.

"They're . . . bowing." Pete's mouth was dry.

"Because we didn't get sick. Is everyone else sick?"

Pete was speechless. Months hard-fought, dodging hordes of Creakers, for a few small parcels of food. Almost lost his life today for a few apples he'd seen on his last travels. Slicing Creaker's throats while she slept. And here they stood. Undisturbed.

"Daddy?"

"Yes, baby?"

"You should follow me."

Pete's feet inched forward. A Creaker spotted him and lurched, sparking others into motion. Pete jumped back. "Christine!"

"No!" Christine thrust her hands out to them. The movement ceased. She walked back to Pete slowly and grabbed his hand. "Come on, Daddy. I think they'll be good."

Pete and Christine walked the quarter mile to the dock where a small boat clung to the melting ice.

"What do we do now, Daddy?"

"I don't know, baby." Pete sat on the snowy ground.

"We can stay here. I don't think they're going to hurt us."

Pete looked longingly back to the lake house. A mass of disjointed faces, of misshapen bodies, peppered the grounds. Hundreds of shattered figures, in fealty to a small child. Their queen.

"I don't want to stay there anymore, Christine." Pete was weak, his fight was lost.

"Daddy? I'm going to make them go, okay? Then we can go home. Okay, Daddy?" She pulled away.

Pete watched the back of her head as she stepped gently back toward the putrid crowd. Christine touched the hair of one. She grabbed it hard.

"Christine no!" Pete shot up, skidding on the wet ground.

"It's okay, Daddy. They come apart really easily. Like the one in the basement." Christine pulled hard, her small hand pressed against the Creaker's shoulder, snapping its head off its body. "See?"

Pete stood terrified.

"Come on, Daddy. It's okay."

Pete didn't move. Christine stared at him. A glare he'd never seen before. A shock of heartlessness in her eyes hit him like a dart to the neck. He staggered back.

"Daddy?"

"Coming, baby." Pete walked slowly behind, pulling grunts from the crowd, and inched next to her, grabbing her slick, bloody hand.

"Aren't they silly, Daddy?" Christine's red, tear-stricken face was replaced with a windswept pink, her eyes full of wonder.

"Yes, Christine. They are."

11

JUSTICE

SHALLOW

GEORGE MELLECK UNFOLDED the torn notebook pages slowly with close examination.

The fury of the pen almost clawed its way through. This letter was cathartic, releasing decades of terror through a ballpoint pen. The scribbling was so poor that George, a spirited author new to The Georgia Post, had to bring the letter to the level of his eyes and turn it sideways. Pages and pages, holding them this way and that for the last few weeks had George's head in a tailspin. Traveling from Chicago to Atlanta for research on the fourth book in his series, *Legends of Terror: Southern Tales of Mayhem*, made George weary. Deciphering what he called 'whacks' from the generational bedtime stories was a task in itself. But there was something inherently strange about the demeanor of the man from Tennessee who traveled the long way to deliver the scrawled story to him, hat in hand. The letter read:

Now, I'm gonna tell it to you like it was told to me, but I've got to change a few names, to protect the innocent and such but also because I still got family here and I don't need to let them know I'm still spooked by this but here we go. And think about changing my name when you're done with all of this, Mister.

"Spooked?" George asked and shook his head, "There's got to be a better word out there."

George became more unnerved as the story unfolded, and against his better judgment, he stylized the scribble into a flowing masterpiece. He'd gone through a few dialect-heavy drafts that he scrapped. The character's dialogue was so messy that they ran the risk of unhinging their jaw. It was time for a rewrite and this one, he loved. He'd actually kissed the paper once it printed out.

Today, he sat in the plush green chair perched near the window of his rented apartment in the widow's peak of a registered county mansion. Rich yellow brocade curtains bookended the antique lace panels that smelled of dust. His fingers rolled across the voice recorder and set it beside him, watching its peaks come alive as he read back his work in question to check for mistakes. He began—

'On a crisp September night in Memphis, Tennessee 1953, Donna Dugan sat bleary-eyed in her claw foot tub with its chipping enamel. With her hair soaked to the sides of her face, she closed her eyes slowly and let the smoke from her long cigarette marinate slowly in her mouth. She exhaled softly, savoring it all. Between her pink polished toes, a murk bled into the steaming water. The putrid bubbling green went unnoticed by a near-napping Donna.

A watery gasp unlocked her eyes. Inches from her face, the gaping mouth of a rotting woman sighed heavily, and the contents of the corpse's mouth drained into Donna's, drowning any hope of a scream. Donna leaped from the tub onto the floor in one ragged breath and turned back only to see a clear pool inside the tub, still steaming.

The usually bright and early Saturday sound of small feet scampering to Sheppard's Creek took over the grass-spotted paths like velvet hammers. A boy was rifling through a small yellow book titled The Hiker's Handbook. Dennis Dugan Jr., DJ to his mama and a few others, was small in stature but lanky in the oddest places. He stood stiffly with a dreamy look in his eye.

'Come on, where is it?' he said. His frustration grew. He flipped harder through the pages and stopped. 'Ah-ha, g-got it.'

DJ read the passage aloud, his stutter taking hold.

'Wet the b-ball of your index finger and point it to the sky. Observe which side of your f-finger feels the coolest. W-w-hichever d-direction the cool side of your finger is facing; that's the direction the w-wind is coming from.' Dennis licked his finger, closed his eyes, and pointed his finger to the sky.

A rustle of twigs and dirt and DJ was pushed from behind, his shoelace catching on a raised tree root, sending him face down into a deep puddle. While trying to steady himself, he slipped back into the puddle with a hard thud.

'Freak!' A taller boy kicked him in his side, making him choke in more water as they watched him struggle. DJ tried to wiggle his fingers into the dirt to lift himself but couldn't. Something in the puddle was clutching at his neck. His pursed lips began to blue from holding his breath, his tight-shut eyes dragged awake from fear. Bits of something yellow floated amongst the algae and caught his eye in the gurgling hum of water. A rotting woman's face surfaced to meet his.

'Help me! Help me!' A mix of gargling rattle and high-pitched clamor splintered through his mind.

As DJ tried to shake free, the woman's grip tightened, drawing him even deeper in. Grabbing his head, she released a scream so piercing it knocked him up and backward out of the water, terrifying the group of bullies. All the chastising had stopped, and at once, the boys scattered throughout the park.

A ring of coral lipstick rimmed a bright yellow coffee cup as a bony hand stirred the black coffee contained in it. The oddly long fingers belonged to Mabel Hammond, neighbor, busy body, bouffantess.

'That boy really shouldn't be in those woods alone.' Mabel's drawl ran muddy with judgment.

Donna ran DJ's clothes through the mangle, teeth tightly gnashed behind pursed lips.

'I won't cage him. He's got to live.'

'He had to have gotten into something else, Donna, these smell like rotten fish.'

'It's odd, isn't it? Never smelled anything like it.'

'Well thank God my Jimmy was out looking for him.'

Donna's hands clenched around the clothes, mangled in frustration. 'Yes, Mabel. Thank God.'

Jimmy Hammond, cradled by enormous glasses, stared mouth agape in the doorway of Dennis's bedroom, afraid. A quiet tremor in his lips. His breath was shallow and quick. DJ twitched in his sleep. Mabel's shouted whisper startled him.

'Honey, get away from that door.'

'Yes, mama.'

DJ's lips quivered, murmuring syllables inaudible to the others. His eyes darted back and forth like a metronome behind his lids. He was slipping in and out of consciousness, stiff and still. And he would lay that way for some time until a sonic boom blasted in his head, sending him somewhere between hell and a dream. In that instant, the scent enveloped him. A stale, muddy scent of cigars and cigarettes, sticky floors, and warm brew hit him square in the face.

He wandered slowly into a room he'd never seen before. A room that shimmered vividly behind reddened eyelids. Couples danced, a man was getting closer and closer to a woman near the jukebox, and a redheaded woman in a yellow chiffon dress canoodled with three men in the corner taking shot after shot from a tall brown bottle. At last, a face he recognized; a jolt pulsed through him, setting every hair on end. Dennis Dugan Sr.- in the flesh. In very, very, healthy and living flesh.

'For she's a jolly good fellow, for she's a jolly good fellow!' The rowdy corner crowd began to sway. The beautiful redhead elbowing Dennis Dugan Sr. in the side had a megawatt smile, melting every heart in the room. Sherry Lavoe was a thunderbolt in a barren field.

'Aww, knock it off, you big palookas.'

'Aw come on, Sherry, one more round a pool before you leave us high and dry!' Jeff Hammond had his eyes buried deep in Sherry's cleavage. Sherry pressed at the front of her dress and straightened her spine.

'No way, I'm a career girl now, official Secretary for Mr. Courtney J. Dalworth Esq. In Chattanooga, Tennessee.'

The crackle of a voice from the corner broke the laughter.

'Official town slut, if you ask me.' Long fingers tapped on the crossed arms of Mabel Hammond who stood squarely behind her husband, Jeff.

'Now wait just a minute!' Dennis pulled Sherry behind him on instinct.

'Don't you think you better get home to your wife too, Dennis? This is a disgrace.'

Sherry pushed her way around the corner table, spilling the remaining contents of the tall brown bottle. 'Who the fuck do you think you are? You got no right!' Mabel broke free from Jeff. A crowd formed slowly in interest.

'I have every right. You waltz into town, borrow our husbands, get yourself in a family way, and skip town as if nothing happened. Now, which one of you did it? Which one?'

Sherry's slap to Mabel came swift and hard, sending Mabel stumbling to the ground. Dennis pulled Sherry, who stood, fists clenched.

'It was you! Dennis Dugan, you louse! Donna's gonna know tonight!'

'You get her on home, Jeff! Git!' Dennis's teeth stayed gritted as his eyes slowly scanned the room. A crowd of commotion closed in on Mabel as Dennis and Sherry sneaked out the back door. Dennis cracked the ignition and peeled out of the gravel parking lot of Duff's Drive-In and Motor Court with Sherry in tow. She sobbed loudly as Dennis drove in silence with one hand on her shoulder.

The radio glow of Dennis's Chrysler Imperial paled him and Sherry in an inhuman light as they turned the car onto the Sheppard Park Overpass.

'They just don't know a thing about me, do they?' Sherry wiped her nose with the back of her hand as she stared straight ahead at the road.

'Nothing they need to know.' Dennis pulled off a breakaway to a small overlook at Sheppard's Creek. He let the car run for a few minutes in silence.

'Courtney loves me. He saw this as the best way. And now that I'm having a baby, I figured, I'm gonna need work.'

'I understand, Sherry, I do.'

'Look, you got a nice family. Donna, she seems real nice and that boy. He's a wonder. So smart. Don't mess things up on account of me.'

'Are you sure you don't need any money?'

'I thought getting rid of this baby was my only option and then Courtney happened, and he said he'd love it just the same.'

'If you change your mind, Sherry.'

'I know.'

'Jeff know it's his?'

Sherry nodded slowly and rubbed her small bump. 'He knows. Tonight's the first he's spoken to me since I told him. I figured it was his idea of a goodbye kiss.'

'I know people don't understand you and the women here are fiery 'cause you're new and shiny. But my mamma was a lot like you. Knew what she wanted in life and knew how to get it. She did the best she could with me. You're smart too. It'll all work out.'

'Thank you, Denny.'

Dennis leaned into Sherry for a small, sad, platonic embrace and rolled down the window. He dislodged a pack of crushed smokes out of his front pocket and turned in the direction of rustling gravel.

'You sonofabitch!'

Dennis fell in Sherry's lap, knocked unconscious by a shotgun barrel. Blood sprayed across the steering wheel in a fan as Sherry tried in vain to cradle his weeping head.

'Get out of the car you tramp!'

Sherry clawed her way into the backseat and kicked violently at the angry hand that grabbed at her. The car door flung open and in the rear-view mirror, a face that had greeted Dennis Jr. with joy at bath time, a warm smile at the breakfast table, Donna Dugan. Donna opened the door wider and dragged Sherry out by her hair and onto the ground.

'Please, please, it's not what you think.' Sherry flailed her hands, her face wet with tears.

Donna reached into the vehicle and pushed aside a bleeding Dennis to put it into neutral. Sherry's eyes affixed to his broken skull, an unfathomable dent at his temple like a stepped-upon soda can.

"Get the fuck out of this car, bitch!"

'No!'

Donna lifted the shotgun quickly. Sherry begrudgingly sidled toward the back of the car.

'Now push.'

'Please don't do this! You don't understand!'

'I will blow a hole clean through your head if you don't shut the hell up and push!'

Sherry dug her heels into the ground and slipped but hurriedly began again. The car loosened and before long took its descent off the overlook, crashing through the vegetation below.

'Now walk!'

Sherry walked into the night, down gnarled and winding paths into the gorge of Sheppard's Creek with Donna Dugan close behind her. As they reached the high and rushing water of the stream, Sherry shivered.

'Get in.' Donna lifted the shotgun to shoulder level and steadied herself against the soft bank.

'Please, Donna, you don't understand, Den didn't do nothing wrong. He ain't never done nothing to me, you got the wrong man!'

'Get. In.'

Sherry stepped into the ice-cold water, sending a loud gasp out into the Tennessee night.

'Just let me go. Tomorrow I'll be out of your lives forever. Just let me go.'

'Oh, you're gonna go, sweetheart. Now turn around, right now!' Donna fired into Sherry's back, catapulting bits of flesh back at her. Sherry toppled forward into the river and was sent meandering down the current. A navy-blue haze took over Donna's face. Darker, darker still. To black.

A ruffle of sheets turned heads in the kitchen and DJ shot straight up in bed, eyes fully rolled back to whites, and let out a scream so guttural it shook the crucifix clean off his bedroom wall. Donna took off like a shot to her son's side. Trying to hold onto him, DJ jerked and pushed away. He clasped his hands to his head and shook violently back and forth. Donna mouthed screams of desperation. Mabel and Jimmy Hammond ran out clutching each other.

Dennis focused on his mother's mouth.

'Please, please! Tell me what happened!' she pleaded.

Dennis opened his mouth to speak, his throat paralyzed. He squirreled back into the headboard, clawing and afraid. In an instant, an odd, dreamy state took over him just as it did by the puddle. Calm. Dennis's eyes rolled down exposing bright blue marbles, only to roll gently back to white as he slumped sideways in a position Donna remembered well. She recoiled for a moment and looked around for a sign of anyone. The boy shook and panted, a small squeak of a sound, his voice a gurgle. He foamed at the mouth that grew wider with every pant. Acrid green water, overrun with decay, poured out of the now gaping cavity of a mouth. The glaring whites of Dennis's eyes silently judged Donna, and he began to speak.

'Wrong man. Wrong man.'

Donna flung backward against the chest of drawers and slid down in a heap. Gasping for air, her eyes wild as he slowly slid down off the bed, onto his stomach, bones crackling and displacing his body in an unnatural undulation.

'Oh God. Oh God.'

DJ slid to face her and vomited heavily. Swamp water, rocks, plastic, and algae covered the floor. He heaved repeatedly and cocked his head back at an angle so violently you could hear his neck snap. What had once been a mouth had grown to the size of his small chest. Fingers came slowly peeking out of Dennis's mouth, followed by a forearm and shoulder. Yellow chiffon clung to matted hair. The puddle woman had returned, and her putrid flesh dislodged itself and fell to the floor. The woman opened her mouth to speak, releasing murk onto the floor near Donna's hands. Donna had adhered herself to the lower dresser drawer. The woman clasped her rubbery fingers tightly around Donna's neck. Her gritted remnants of teeth grinned wickedly as she swiftly dragged Donna down into the liquid mess purged onto the floor.

Dennis jerked and shook, his body finally coming to a still, tight fetal position. His features soft, like a sleeping newborn. And there he stayed, sweating, peaceful.

The cold feeling of wet fabric brushed his forehead. Dennis wrenched awake.

'Easy, easy. It's okay.' Donna wrung out a cool washcloth into the small basin.

He read his mother's lips. There was something different about her now, her smile was softer. Her hair had a slight reddish hue. A dance in her eyes brought a caring sweetness that had been missing.

'You gave me a scare. Fell and got knocked down. Hit yer head.'

Dennis nodded in compliant agreement.

'Well, you rest now, Shug. I just got some bread out of the oven. We'll have some when you feel up to it.'

Dennis stared blankly at a smiling Mabel Hammond at the kitchen table. She waved politely at him. Donna walked out of his room, grabbed a carving knife out of the holder, smiled, and closed the door. Dennis curled up tightly. A rasping scream echoed from the kitchen.'

George gasped and inhaled sharply through his nose, clutching the recorder with wet palms. 'Whoo! Scared myself! I think that's closer to the letter.'

He struggled to grip the recorder tighter as it slipped onto the floor. George leaped from his chair, scrambling to grab it. He held it tightly to his chest, now soaked in perspiration. The story had touched him. Not in the tenderness of a feel-good, all's-well-that-ends-well homage but in the hideously invasive calling to learn more. And more and more. The tale had permeated him.

He unscrewed his metal water bottle and gulped from deep thirst. He eyed the last page of the letter, its edges flickering gently in the September breeze that crept under the window sash—

Now that's all I know because that's what the Dugan boy told me. I can take responsibility where it's due, but I can't hold on to this one day more than today. So, you can take this wherever you gotta go Mr. Melleck from the Georgia Post. Tell whomever you like. Tell 'em it's all a lie, tell 'em it's truth I don't care.

I just can't carry it no more. I had to hide after my wife was killed, me and the boy, change states, names, everything. Couldn't pin nothing on me, but I couldn't stand the looks, the talk. So, take it. I'm too old to run, so here I'll sit. She'll come find me, eventually.

Signed Sincerely,
Clive Undercutt nee Jeffrey Elijah Hammond

'Jeff, you piece of shit. All this time.' George dragged his finger along the recorder screen to the start and clicked play. A warble and wheeze choked from it.

'Dammit! No!' It slipped again from his grasp, this time tumbling to the floor and shattering. George knelt in despair. The floor was beaded with moisture. He slid his hand across it, twisting the liquid between his fingers. He pulled them to his face, gagging.

'Oh God!'

The cracks in the floorboards began to bleed a thick green serum, growing heavy, flooding the floor. Clapped footsteps lumbered behind George as he whimpered softly.

'Please. No God, please no.'

A thick watery voice cut the room sharply. 'George?'

'Please God, no!'

Two rancid arms grasped him close. Greasy and bloated hands fumbled around his mouth and clasped it closed. Decaying yellow fabric swayed in the breeze, mingling with the brocade panels. His eyes grew large and began to weep as his muffled screams created bubbles between festering fingers.

She breathed heavily in his ear. 'Find Jeff.'

The rich yellow brocade curtains snapped shut.

George Melleck awoke sharply and sat on his knees, grasping at his head in pain, sobbing woefully. He rolled over to clean, dry floorboards. Stumbling up, George gagged and choked. Reaching his fingers into his mouth, dislodging a thin yellow strip of chiffon.

George Melleck quit *The Georgia Post* the following day and returned to his small high-rise apartment in Chicago. And as hard as he tried, until the day he took his own life, he could not locate a Mr. Clive Undercutt or Jeffrey Elijah Hammond in any city report in the whole United States.

12

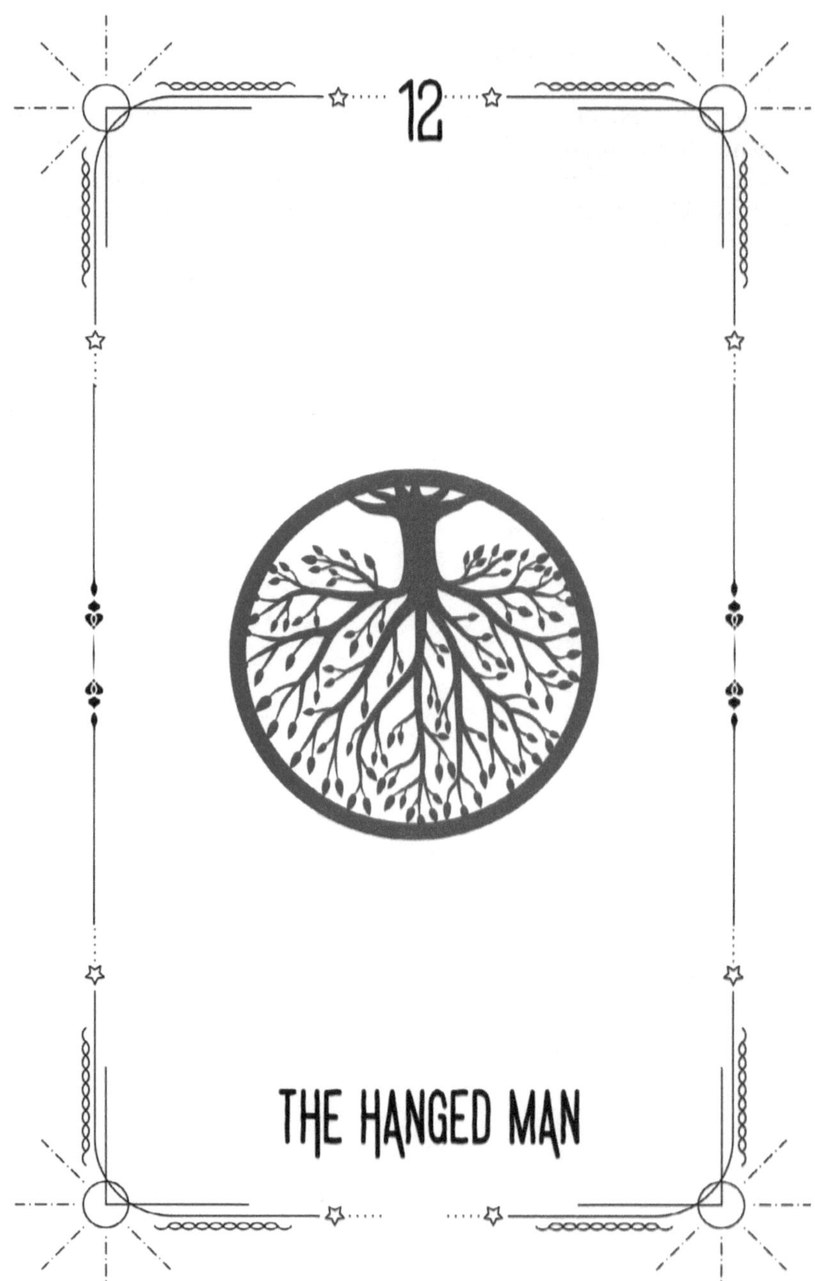

THE HANGED MAN

THE HUMAN SEED

'**I**F WE CAN get the sun from that angle to where I look like a saint, Ted, that'd be perfect. How do I look?'

Charlotte Stanton, evening news anchor, parts her hair in the middle at the back and pulls both sections forward to swing around her shoulders. She's hoping to blow the lid off the 'Government Death Trade.' Or at least that's what she wants to call this piece. Edward in PR thinks 'Dearly Departed or Cold-Hearted?' is a catchier title.

'Damn near godly.' Ted Copes wants to get home to feed the dog. He's hoping for ninety minutes, tops. Adjusting the lens, he motions to Charlotte and mimes the countdown.

'In 3, 2 . . . '

Charlotte readies herself for live television. Unfettered by the dust, noise, and gusts in her direction, she walks along a stretch of the main highway, never glancing away from the camera.

'Dearly departed or cold-hearted? Who's really at the heart of the government death trade?'

'Clear!' Ted smirks. 'One for old Ed?'

'Yep! Okay over here, in 5, 4.' Ted steadies the camera; a beam of sunlight hits her just right.

'Five years ago, not fifteen miles from here, The W.H.O. met with President Hovestandt, several select members of Congress, and Surgeon General Coffey to discuss the beginning stages of what has now become The Arbor Act.'

Charlotte steps forward in earnest.

'The Arbor Act, on the surface, states that ground casket burials are against the law. Mainly due to the population skyrocketing from what was famously known as the Winter Storm Boom of 2025 causing drastic food shortages, the likes that haven't been seen since 1943, and most cities' infrastructures are in crisis. That coupled with climate change rapidly spreading fatal fungi to many deciduous trees, the Act's end game seemed like the proper remedy. The statute of this act was that any deceased was to be buried in an ECOPOD. ECOPODs are functional bio-friendly packages to carry human remains; those remains are then mixed with genetically enhanced plant life. This new system not only creates more vegetation throughout the surface of the planet but also gives back thousands of acres of landscape. Today I spoke with Artie Blank, President and CEO of The Human Seed, Inc., an ECOPOD company, on the lucrative deal he has made with the United States Government.'

Ted slowly claps. 'And cut! Let's move it out!'

'Nice to get it on the horizon like that.' Charlotte turns. Saplings and new trees grow timidly near the metal stalagmites. Skyscraper after skyscraper lines the area behind the highway.

Across town, in a stark white space peppered with succulents of many sizes, Artie Blank stares out the main window of his office. All of six-foot-four, impeccably dressed, and fully white-bearded. And as of late, graced with knees as weak as a dried leaf. He's just finished signing multiple checks. Ten thousand to this one, four hundred thousand to that one.

You can't take it with you, he thinks, and at that moment, all the zeros ceased to matter. These last five years had been the most luxurious, ostentatious, and in closing, the most awe-inspiring and wicked time of his fifty-one-year life.

It's no secret that The Human Seed's exclusive government contract made Artie an incredibly rich man. But you see, in twenty minutes, under the guise of pushing the propaganda of The Arbor Act on a national level, Artie will sign his own death warrant.

He clears his throat and checks his watch. 1:47 pm.

His wife Brenda will be at The Lasko Country Club with her friends. His only child, Aila, will be one hour and thirteen minutes away from the end of her final shift at the hospital before maternity leave. A tight clench in his throat has him heaving, and he quickly bends over the pristine desk to the intercom and waves his hand over the sensor.

'Elise?'

'Yes Artie?'

'Could you pop in for a second?'

Elise Fanahan bounds in with more vigor than she's had in months. Today is her last full day before a solo vacation. Her first vacation alone since the passing of her husband in April.

'Yes, Commander?'

Grabbing the stack of bright yellow envelopes and a surety book, he checks his watch a second time. 'I just need to mail these overnight and place these seven bonds to wire.'

'Who ya payin' off, moneybags?

'Just investing, Elise. Time to consider the future.'

'Just kidding, I know. Grandbaby. I'll take care of it.'

'Elise, Charlotte Stanton, WCTV is coming with a crew today. Send her forward when she arrives. No waiting, I'm decent.'

'You the boss, Boss.'

Artie checks his watch again. 1:52 pm. Just as he was about to sit down and have a nice quiet cry to himself, Elise popped back in.

'She's early.'

'Send her in in five.'

Charlotte's angle is to grill him on the length of the government contract and how he had muscled similar companies out of the market. Making him look more like the bureaucrat he rallied against as opposed to the earth-loving hippie-dip he posed as at the start of the company. She craves the panicked expression of her interviewees, especially men, but this one was going to be different. Artie already had a look of heavy defeat in his eyes and exhaled loudly. He heads over to the bar. Shoving ice into the glass, he begins to pour bottled water but settles for the neighboring scotch. Gulping it down swiftly, he glances at his watch again. 1:55 pm.

Charlotte appears in the doorway like a bird of prey. She saunters in, shooting daggers at Ted, who is still licking his fingers from waiting room chocolates. Ted clears his throat. She reaches out to shake Artie's hand, her fist on top, power move. He grasps it and places his other hand over hers, giving it a slight tap.

'Charlotte, I'm so glad you're here. We've got a lot to discuss and in a very short time.'

'I'm sorry Mr. Blank, short?' Charlotte shoots a panicked look at Ted. 'We agreed to an hour.'

'I'm sorry, but as I continue, you will agree that time is not only of the essence, but my situation will require me to expedite my departure.'

Ted begins to shakily attach the mics to Charlotte's brooch and Artie's tie. He's not going to hear the end of this. This is her David Frost moment and Artie'd gone and fucked it up.

Artie checks the time. 1:58. 'Aila.' He sighs.

Her quizzical eyes meet Artie's gaze. She sits down and motions to Ted to give her ten seconds.

'Ready, Mr. Blank?'

'Yes. Artie, please.'

'4 . . . 3 . . . 2 . . . ' Ted crouches back behind his camera.

'Mr. Blank, you've said The Human Seed company came from very modest beginnings. Do you attribute your company's enormous growth to this new contract with the U.S. Government?'

'Well, Charlotte, I attribute it to the fact that the U.S. Government has a lot of money for the things it wants to concentrate on at any given time. Population, global warming, climate change. The government saw The Human Seed as a healthy alternative. They can be manufactured quickly, one every minute. Death doesn't wait.'

Artie sits back in his office chair and crosses his hands over his ankle, which sits awkwardly on his thin thigh.

'Healthy? Interesting way to put that, Mr. Blank. So how much was that contract?'

'I would say the minutiae of that contract is fully available to you should you want to sit down to thirty-one pages of cans, cannots, and must-dos. Now if you are here under some exposé guise, and I hope you are, I'll need us to take a different direction.'

Charlotte bristled. 'Fair enough, go on.'

'My signing with the U.S. Government in conjunction with the Arbor Act was a no-brainer. Not only from a money standpoint but on a global scale. Casket burial was the greatest racket to ever pray on the most vulnerable human emotion. Vice President Herman Nichols approached me with interest first. His daughter was dying from Lupus and casket, or cremation, was out of the question in her eyes. She majored in Thanatology at Stanford and Vice President Nichols, a simple Baptist man, unfamiliar with the apparent past barbarities of human burial, couldn't understand her indignance. She had been researching my company for quite a while and of course, I agreed to meet with him.'

'So, Artie, where does the contract come in?' Charlotte's lips purse as Artie dances about the question.

'Our conversation drifted into the benefits of the pods. Small, affordable, your choice of plant life mix and safely biodegradable, not to mention better for the environment and space-saving since it's vertical. He then approached President Hovestandt with the information.'

'So that conversation changed history, you could say.' Charlotte flings her raven hair over her shoulder. Power move two. If she could pull all seven, she is looking at Pulitzer territory.

'Indeed. The Arbor Act was passed and put into immediate action seven months later. I could tell it to you backward and forwards.'

'Oh please, I'd love to hear it. As you know, the layman only gets the first blush and then the command. Could you share it, Artie?'

Artie sighs and then smiles with only his lips. She is wasting time. Precious time. Precious time for precious people. Precious to someone, surely all were.

'The Arbor Act of 2035 states that all citizens of the United States of America are hereby prohibited from ground burial in receptacles containing wood, steel, metal, precious metals, and cloth of any kind. Those who are found to violate this law beyond April 30th, 2035, will be exhumed and cremated at the expense of next of kin or guardian. Citizens are advised to be buried in an ECOPOD supplied by The Human Seed, Inc. Any other brand or off-brand is strictly forbidden. Citizen's burial plots will be logged with pod serial numbers to qualify for protection under the National Forest Act which states that final resting places within government-registered forests are protected from upheaval, destruction, fire, and movement due to infrastructure guidelines. Citizens previously buried, with the consent of next of kin, are to be exhumed immediately for the interment exchange. If the citizen has no next of kin, the remains will be cremated and stored in a government-sanctioned storage facility compliant with health standards. The End.'

Charlotte winced at the coldness of the phrase. '*The End?* So, we're supposedly saving the environment and using less space to bury our dead. You've changed the world, Mr. Blank. But I can't help thinking you've single-handedly wiped out the entire casket industry and created what sounds like registered body farms.'

'You would be correct, Charlotte. And before I trouble you further with my ramblings, I have a question for you. Have you ever given any thought to how this curbs the population?'

Charlotte pulls on her hair a bit as her front teeth find the side of her bottom lip. Damn. She is losing it. She is the aggressor. Back on track. She straightens her spine and tilts her chin upwards.

'I hadn't thought about it. I just assumed that it created more space to live, not necessarily fixing the population.'

'Most citizens would say the same thing. Lather, rinse, repeat. No harm no foul. We've saved the day.'

Artie pats himself on both shoulders and lets out a small giggle. And as quickly as it came, his expression meanders to misery.

'Yesterday I was given a bit of sour news that unfortunately is the factor that will cut this interview short. There is an addendum to The Arbor Act titled The Harvest Clause. It states that on a five-year rotation, if there are no deaths in your immediate or extended family of five or larger, there is a volunteer system enacted. This system is dedicated to disposing of one human from each family in the United States to curb the population. The volunteer system has three criteria: status, occupation, and contribution to society. If the citizens do not comply, the government will exterminate one of their choosing.'

Charlotte turns to Ted, mortified. Ted slowly lowers the camera. Charlotte sharply points for him to stay on Artie. 'You can't be serious! This is a farce, and a sick one at that, Mr. Blank!'

'Artie or Mr. Blank, choose one. Charlotte, I'm going to need you to find Mr. Stephen Joahue in the Surgeon General's office. He'll be expecting your call.'

Charlotte stands fervently, knocking the office chair askew. Frost be damned.

'But that's murder! Why would the U.S. Government believe that the only way to solve this is to murder its citizens? And children! Children have no status, no occupation! Think about what you're asking me to tell the American people.'

'Death is big business, Charlotte. Surely in your field, you know that. It's all about control. This environment thing? I'm just a front. A pawn. Save the planet and they'll stop asking questions. Isn't that what everyone wanted? If the government would just pay attention to climate change.' Artie gestures around the room.

Charlotte begins to tear up. Artie's eyes reddened. She stiffens her stance, sniffles once, and is back at it.

'How did you come to find out about this so-called addendum?' Charlotte tries in vain to steady her voice.

'Mr. Joahue reluctantly briefed me less than twenty-four hours ago. We are days away from our first rotation. And I've had to make some very difficult decisions. How do you choose to send one of your own to slaughter?'

'Days?! Why have they not said anything!'

'I told you. Death is big business. This first harvest will be involuntary, a test. A scare tactic. It will be made to look like a terrorist invasion. One on a scale you can never imagine.'

Artie takes a large inhale. Ted sets the camera on the desk and sits down heavily on the carpet, pale.

'Now Charlotte, please, call Mr. Joahue. He's got a copy of the addendum. Blow this open. Blow this whole thing to shreds. Please go now!'

Charlotte, on instinct, grabs Artie by the lapels and over-corrects scurrying back from him. 'And where will you go? They will come after you for this!'

Artie slowly backs away from Charlotte with tears in his eyes. Ted watches them through the screen of the camera. 'Charlotte, thank you for your time. Now if you'll excuse me, I have some volunteer work to do.'

And with that, Artie Blank turns on his heel to face the large window and places his right hand over his heart for a moment. He inhales, pulls a small handgun out of his jacket pocket, holds it to his temple, and fires.

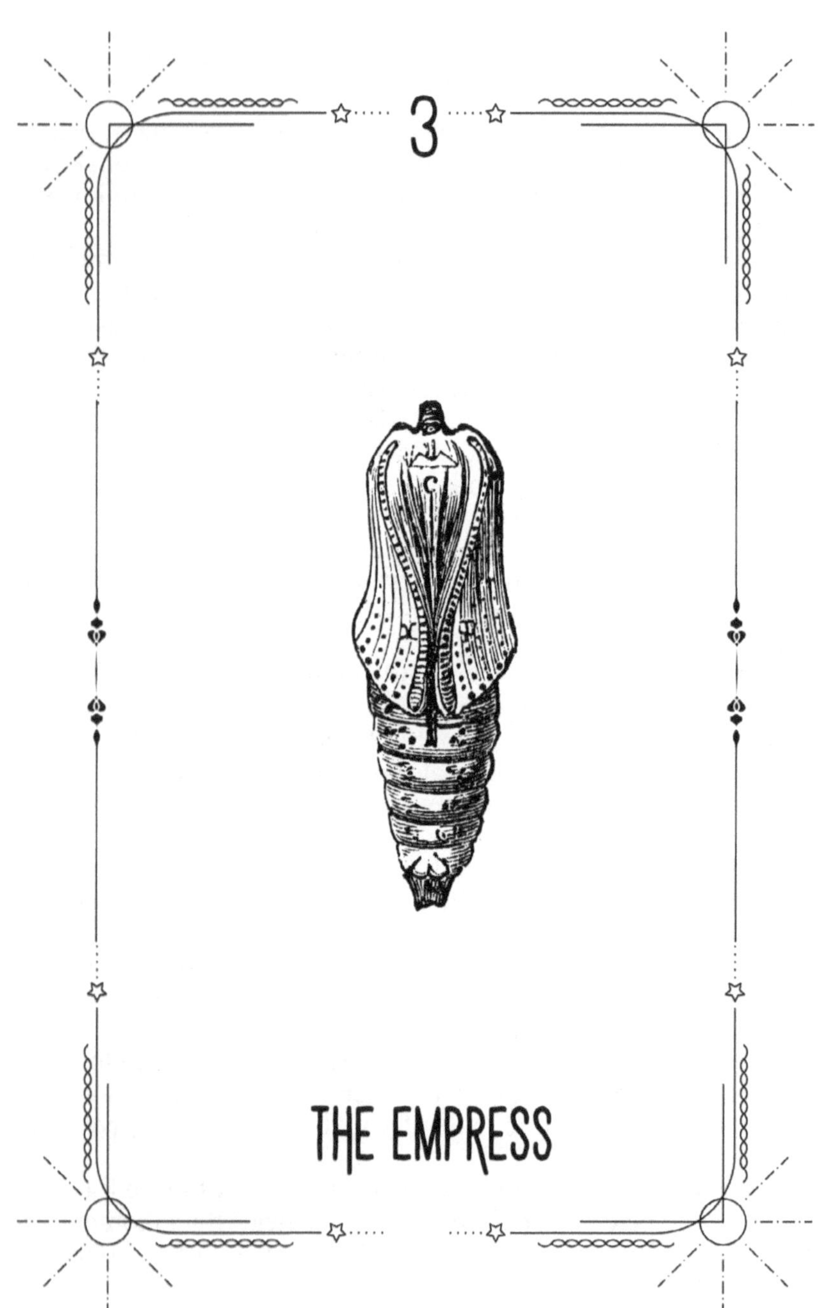

3

THE EMPRESS

MOURNING CLOAK

A PAPER-MÂCHÉ STROLLER dangled gingerly from the drop ceiling. Celia Pegg, newly twenty-five as of today, not that anyone cared, watched from behind thick-walled glasses as a singular shredded pink streamer flitted in the gust of the recycled office air.

'Christ. Celia!'

She startled and narrowed her eyes at the hot pink sugary confection thrust in front of her.

'Hello? Did you want some cake?' Janet Molloy, Operations Manager at Simmons and Simmons Law Firm, was exasperated; her molded blonde hairdo flickered, almost immune to the office airflow.

'Oh, yes! Thank you.' Celia took the plate and fork and placed them on her lap.

'You okay in there? I've been asking you for the last two minutes.' Janet pursed her lips and began to clear the cake table.

'Yes, I was just thinking, is all. What a beautiful spread, Janet. So nice of you to do this for Meghan.'

'Well, yes, this is our first office baby. Enough weddings already, am I right?' Janet gathered the ends of the plastic tablecloth and wound it into a ball.

'I wouldn't know, Janet. I don't get invited to those kinds of things.' Celia placed a piece of cake in her mouth.

Janet glared as the gummy pink glaze danced around Celia's braces like taffy. She stifled a slight gag and turned away quickly.

'Well, I'm sure your time will come.' Janet smiled gently and shuffled off, leaving Celia to eat alone as the rest of the office convened in the conference room. Watching from the crack in the conference room door, Celia's mind wandered. It had been doing that a lot lately.

She pictured pulling pink taffeta-lined dresses out of bursting glossy bags riddled with chubby-faced animals, of shaking yellow rattles to smiles and claps from the office folk. Even the curmudgeonly Jim, head of abstracts, was particularly thrilled. Envisioning taking in the room, Celia stood at the head of the long conference table adorned with pink paper plates and baby carriage confetti among the piles of tissue paper.

'Thank you, thank you all for coming and celebrating my baby. I'm so excited to meet her, I just can't wait. It's been such a lovely experience.' Celia rubbed at her belly in a full dream state. Something hard hit her face, startling her out of her fantasy. A crumpled heap of a gift bag hit the floor.

'What the hell, you creep?!' Jim stood red-faced.

Celia's eyes darted around, bewildered. She'd wandered into the conference room, to the head of the table. Her hand firmly grasped Meghan's belly. Meghan sat stunned and teetered on the verge of a full-blown sob.

'Get her off of me!' Meghan whispered to the room.

Janet rose swiftly and pulled Celia out of the room to the sounds of taunts and shouts. Jim crowded Meghan, who began to howl.

Celia edged against the wall and Janet's grip tightened. She thrust Celia down in a cubicle office chair firmly.

'Celia, honestly, what a spectacle! What's the matter with you?' Janet dialed zero from the desk phone. Janet was panting, her face reddening as well.

Celia ran her tongue across her teeth—still caked with pink frosting. She grabbed a tissue from the desk Kleenex box and turned, furiously scrubbing at her teeth.

'I didn't mean to upset Meghan, honest.'

'It was a disgusting display, Celia, just ridiculous. You really ought to see someone.' Janet turned her attention away from Celia. 'Yes? Hello Henry, Janet Molloy here, could I have an employee meeting with you? We've had a bit of a disturbing day.'

Celia began to speak but Janet held her hand up to Celia's face, sealing her fate.

Janet hung up the phone with a sigh. 'Come with me, Celia.'

Walking grimly past the now full desks of fellow employees, Celia shuddered. Jim stood angrily at his corner office entrance and huffed a muttered, 'God damn freak.'

"That'll be all, Jim." Janet pulled Celia along.

Celia had been watching a butterfly flit anxiously outside the office window of Henry Fallton, Head Counselor of Simmons and Simmons, as he prattled on about office correctness and decorum. Its graceful glide and its antsy wings gave her a wry smile.

'Ms. Pegg, I'm afraid we've got to let you go.'

'Mr. Fallton?' Celia's eyes pleaded for a bit and returned to the butterfly that seemed to perch on the screen behind Fallton's left shoulder.

'It's not that we don't value your contribution here, Ms. Pegg, it's just that this has been a qualifying incident for dismissal. We've got seven other complaints about, um, personal hygiene, disorderly conduct, topics of conversation making other employees uncomfortable, and stalking complaints. Ms. Pegg, I'm not sure how we would, in good conscience, keep you on.'

'You're beautiful.' Celia stared wistfully at the butterfly now higher on the screen.

'Miss Pegg!'

Celia's spine straightened tight as her attention snapped back to Fallton.

Fallton heaved a heavy groan and looked at Celia earnestly. 'You have exactly ten minutes to clean out your area. An escort will be waiting by your desk to keep you on time. I do hope you find the help you need.'

'I don't need any help, Mr. Fallton. Simply better people to work around, perhaps.'

Celia stood and took one last longing look at the butterfly and stepped out of the office.

After spending three days watching television, volleying between *Snapped* and The Cooking Channel, Celia ventured out into the world—the wide and bright world of horn honks and shoes on dusty and broken sidewalks—to Raven's Butterfly Sanctuary. The Sanctuary had always calmed her, its lithe swaying nature of tall grass that jutted out against the bright pink peony flowers. The red brick pathway meandered through the domed park in splinters like capillaries.

Celia took the old maintenance exit, now abandoned due to the recent extension. It departed onto a tree-arched pathway, shutting out the sky and creating a night scene in the middle of the day.

Celia walked slowly, admiring the makeshift canopy above her. She stopped short as a low buzz snatched the air from around her.

Sidling slowly around the edge of the building, she noticed a man's body lying on the ground in a contorted position, like a crash test dummy. Inching closer, his face came into view. A gaping hole sat atop hunched shoulders and a punctured torso. His neck, clearly broken, was being siphoned slowly. Her gaze followed the source of the siphon spout in disbelief: the fidgeting and extended proboscis of a human-sized butterfly. Its legs clattered about the man's body, seeming to tenderize him, its spiracle gyrating wildly.

Celia drew her hand to her mouth quietly and watched it feed. Its wings undulated delicately behind its body. A sour juxtaposition to the frenzy of its feast. In a flutter, it lifted its head and caught Celia's gaze, and as she opened her mouth to scream, the butterfly charged her, rapping its bulging head against her face and knocking her to the ground. A distant car horn sent the butterfly straight up in a shot, slicing Celia's face with its wing.

Celia sat speechless, weeping silently, and fumbling at the deep cut on her cheek. She stood slowly, walked over to the remnants of the man, and stepped over him. She continued her even pace along the arched alleyway, up the stairs to the street.

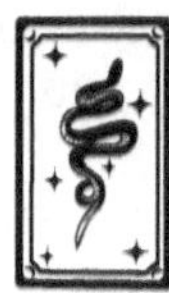

Sporting nine new stitches on her left cheek, Celia entered the arched alleyway again, two days after the 'feast of the man.' She had been referring to the incident as that in her journal along with small doodles of Janet Molloy with roaches in her helmet hair. The strong summer breeze made her cheek smart, and it glistened with ointment in the sun. She had given a spirited account to the attending nurse about a mugger who had sliced her as something to remember him by. As the nurse laced Celia's last stitch, she wished her well and told her of a place that sold off-market stun guns.

Finding her way back to the place of the feast, Celia felt a pang of regret, of remorse even. Not for the man, no, but for the gorgeous creature she'd frightened away. The man's body was gone, fully. A large maroon puddle lay in the corner and disappeared in a mass of gelatinous strings that bounded up into the rafters of the back end of the maintenance building. It glistened like a thousand Fourth of July sparklers in the small peeks of daylight and twisted its sticky spindles in the soft breeze under thickening rain clouds. Celia's eyes followed the glass-like entrails to a leafy brown sack that flickered anxiously against the rafter edge. It took the shape of a drooping tulip, head down as if ashamed. Mesmerized, Celia stepped into the viscous puddle. The sack twitched, alarming her, and sending her body backward and down into the sappy pond. She slid against the low point of the building with a thud.

Looking up at the sack, she pushed her hand to her mouth and shrieked. A tiny foot jerked from within the pouch. A tiny human foot. With five little toes, as they should be. Celia pushed herself up to the side of the building to stand beneath it. She brushed her finger lovingly against it in a small spiral pattern. The sack fluttered wildly.

'Oh, you like that? You sweet thing.'

Balancing herself against the building, Celia fumbled inside her satchel for her house keys.

'You can't be out here all by yourself.' And with a hyper sawing motion, Celia freed the sack from the wall and web and tendrils. The sack twisted in her hands, and she held it gingerly as she placed it in her satchel.

A baby, it's got to be, she thought.

Celia crept along the building wall to dry asphalt and placed her satchel on the ground. Turning her long coat inside out, she placed it back on, wincing at the damp fabric against her skin. She carried her satchel lovingly against her and walked up the steps to the street.

Seated in a sea of soft pink blankets sat the brown sack in a shoddy wicker bassinet on wheels. Celia had washed the sack off gently and now began to rock it back and forth. She'd been researching larvae pods and growth time. Her eyes bounded around a page of large print.

LARVAE GESTATIONAL PERIOD—4 DAYS

Celia's eyes grew large. Her gaze fell upon the muddy brown bulge in the cheap bassinet. How long had it been since the man feast? Two? Three days? She stroked it lovingly, then twisted her body to grab it with both hands. Its outer shell cracked under the pressure.

'No! Oh no!' Celia began to whimper.

Bits of cracked shell tumbled like sugar glass onto her lap in a million shards and pieces. She screamed, cried, and tried to place it back into the bassinet gently. It pulled and pulsated beneath her hands, and she spat and shrieked as it shifted crudely in its basket.

'No! Baby no! I'm sorry!' She knelt by the bassinet in fear. Abruptly, the noise ceased. All but a small whip crack. Celia's eyes peered sheepishly over the side of the bassinet. She stood slowly, her face growing greyer and greener the taller she became. She reached her hand out to the tiny human foot and stroked it. It hissed ferally. She did it again and it rolled its pulpy body toward her hand.

For there were no other human feet. Just one small human foot fused into a bulbous spiracle that twitched along with seven other prolegs. She ran her finger up its sticky body to its head. Its true legs grabbed her finger gently, in the unconscious movement of an infant in comfort. In its head capsule sat two peering human eyes of blue. Celia pulled her hand back and froze.

Quite vividly, the memory of her seventh birthday flooded into her mind as the prolegs tickled at her fingers. From that birthday onward, Celia always requested a Cinderella cake with a sparkling candle. With her mother's hand on her shoulder and across the table from one of the neighborhood girls who was forced to come, Celia made her wish. To be a mother. It was a silly thing for a young girl to wish for and it would be something she'd wish for every year until she was twenty. Her mother would die that year. Forty-three days after they shared their last piece of light blue Cinderella cake. The wish had been packed away in this house, in the attic, amongst the dust and cobwebs, amongst the play kitchen and collectible Barbies her father said he'd get to pricing one day. A box within a box within a box. Taped wholly and buried.

But today, for Celia, it was a gift.

Celia pursed her lips and blew, like so many other candles and dreams and hopes and wishes. She wrapped the blankets in a swaddle around her baby and picked it slowly out of the bassinet to her chest. She looked into its deep blue eyes and smiled. Celia gasped in happiness. She pulled the baby away to stare at it in awe once more. A small crack started on its left mandible and slowly crept to the right, the sinew on each jaw hinge pulled desperately on itself. A large slit lay angrily across the baby's head. A jaw filled with tiny teeth lunged itself into Celia's chest and she roared uncontrollably. Its mouth twisted and tangled, then settled. Celia crumpled in on herself as the baby suckled heartily.

As the days passed, the larvae wiggled their way out of the bunting and writhed beneath the baby blanket adorned with chubby-faced animals. Its high-pitched shrieks had become a slow pulsing symphony to Celia as she wandered befuddled to the bassinet. She neither loved it nor hated it. She felt dutiful, chosen at that. Getting the proverbial nod from the universe.

Celia's skin had been yellowing, bruising easily. She was tired; her breasts were rank from infection and pressure. The parental bonding of bloodletting had pulled her into a hypervigilance of protection. Her baby would have everything she could give until she couldn't give it again. She would proceed today, like the last twenty-six days, in earnest, with the daily feed.

Rolling the blanket beneath its glutinous body, she shushed it softly though it did not hear, it did not comply and would not until the slit in its malformed head would be filled. And as she calmed its insatiable need, each suckle felt harder, longer, as though life itself was drifting quietly through her veins. Sailing from this world and onto the next. And with that, she gave the larvae a slight pull closer to her. Celia parted her dry, husk-laden lips, let out a labored sigh, and smiled.

'It's been such a lovely experience.'

THE WHEEL

RUMPUS

THE FIRST NIGHT was awful. I've been living here for a very long time and always welcomed new and interesting people into my space. It was easy, you see, just come right in and I'll be very amenable to your personality and needs and idiosyncrasies and such, but never any extreme bending because, as I've stated, it's my space. But never in all my days of waiting and waking, walking the house through the day, and hiding out for another round of the moon, have I ever been so terrified of a guest as I am now.

You don't have much of a choice in my line of work. You play the cards you are dealt. You invite them in, and they stay, quietly and pleasantly, and you miss them, sometimes terribly, when they go. Sometimes they make horrible messes, or you have horrible fights, and they leave just as quickly as they came. Some come and ignore you completely. That is the way. That's the way it has been for me, for the last hundred and seventy-nine years since my death.

But as I said before, the first night was awful. She came, bouncing in as they usually do, eyes darting around their new surroundings. Their new hideaway. We locked our eyes immediately, and that's when I knew. She was going to be trouble. Most times it takes a few days for them to notice me. Some stare, some shudder, some shun. Most of the time, they force themselves to disregard me completely. She stared at me, almost looking directly through me, and then stepped forward.

'I see you,' she said. 'Come out, all the way out.' She stepped closer. I turned, allowing her to take in what she could of me.

'You're not gonna stay here. Not if I can help it.'

I like these kinds of challenges. The ornery ones that took charge on the first step inside. I'd rearrange their surroundings while they were out. Whisper murderous thoughts in their ears while they slept. Pull open the closet door two inches wider than where they'd left it. They'd crumble within days. But Cindy, that's her name, did what no guest has ever done. She whispered back to me.

Whispered things of unnatural origin. Of her slaying others like me in other corners of the world where she slept or took refuge. She told me about her 'unfortunate mistakes' when it came to animals and how they always seemed to die not long after she got them and how she would make a terrible fuss and become despondent in front of the elder guests, so much so they would buy her just about anything, anything at all. In fact, they've bought her my home. Right out from under me.

I'd been quiet for a while you see, minding my own business. I suppose they thought no one would mind. They had traveled far, on account of her brother Andrew tragically falling out the window in their last home. She'd been watching him, while her parents painted his room and furnished it with beautiful shiny things and fish, three brightly colored fish in separate bowls. She'd wanted fish for a very long time. Longer than Andrew had even been alive, she said. She wanted a new pink room but had been told to wait. She might outgrow the 'little girl' things, her father had said. Her bed creaked and swayed and the spindle at the top of one of the bedposts was loose. And at that, she had also been told to wait. She didn't want to wait any longer.

Andrew had been watching birds. His chin barely skimmed the window ledge as he watched the hummingbirds flit out and about and he giggled loudly and pushed ever so slightly against the sill trying to reach them. Cindy had gone to the kitchen to make them sandwiches when she heard a loud crash. Andrew had fallen out of the window onto a glass lawn table in the yard, she said. She stared at me for many moments as if trying to trace every inch of my face in her mind.

'Pity,' she said. 'I didn't know he could climb.'

She grew harried and manic at his death, she said.

Telling the elder guests that she should have waited to make the sandwich, but Andrew was pleading and hungry and they were busy, and she was big now and shouldn't need help. And oh, how the elders grew so dedicated and eager to please her. Holding onto the house they shared with Andrew was unthinkable. So here they came at her request. To the top floor of the most beautiful old apartment building in all of New York City.

My city. My home. My room. She has taken it all from me. I was here first. As a spirit, I was solitary. But guests have opened my eyes to the vastness of evil that runs through the lathe and plaster, through the modern electrical wires, and I became more. So much more. I grew from tales of wicked things and ghosts of old guests, and old blood in the grooves of the floor. I'm built of strands of hair hundreds of years old, painted into these walls, the same walls that house dozens of bodies, unknown to most. I'm anything and everything you fear, and hope can't be real with every hair that stands up on your trembling hull. I am a phantom. And she can see me as plain as any piece of furnishing in this room.

And here I sit trembling, on day forty-seven of Cindy's stay. She whispers to me at night of all her atrocities and sicknesses like a deranged and odious Aesop. Night after night. Until today. She spoke about how a very rich banker and her father have become great friends. He likes the way she plays piano. He wishes he had a little girl like her. He is old, grey-bearded, and happy. His apartment is bigger and grander and taller than this one. She's going to go outside tomorrow and play before the elder guests wake up, and she will turn all the gas on and close the door tightly.

The elder guests never awoke and several men in yellow suits came to clear their belongings. On the very last day of Cindy, she stood in the doorway of my grand house clutching the hand of the grey-haired man, weeping slowly. As they turned to leave, her ruddy face gave me the largest grin, and her chubby pink fingers danced in the air as she said goodbye.

You would think I'd be happy to be rid of her. Back to the old song and dance. But I can't. She's tainted it, more than the grey-haired man. My darling home of almost two centuries. I will find another quiet and old territory with stories and history built into its walls and stroked into its plaster. I will take no more guests as I have no more fight. She has broken me as she has broken others, and with that knowledge, I will think no more of her.

She will try to destroy the old grey man as well. Another grander, taller apartment. Another monster to defeat. But not for her. Because I know what the old grey man used to do when he was a guest in my home, whose bodies he hid in this place.

And she will soon know and join the others that I'm sure line the walls of his new tall, grand apartment.

ABOUT THE CONTRIBUTORS

Mo Moshaty is a writer, lecturer, and producer. She has incorporated her extensive Horror background, as well as her career as a Cognitive Behavioral Therapist, into lectures with Prairie View A&M in Texas as a keynote speaker for *Nightmares from Monkeypaw: A Jordan Peele Symposium*; Miskatonic Institute of Horror Studies on *From Inside the House: Dissecting Women's Trauma in Horror,* and *The Whole Damn Swarm: 30 Years of Candyman* with University of Sheffield; Fear2000 for *The Horror Evolution Will Be Colorized*; and many more.

She is a core member and producer with Nyx Horror Collective, whose *13 Minutes of Horror* Film Festival screened on Shudder; of Stowe Story Labs, a collective focused on supporting woman-identifying creatives over 40 working in the Horror genre; and she is the Editor-in-Chief of NightTide Magazine.

Mo featured in *160 Black Women in Horror* by Sumiko Saulson, Kenya Moss-Dyme, and Kai Leakes. Her short fiction has appeared in numerous venues, and her novella, *Love the Sinner* (Brigids Gate), was released in 2022.

Beginning in 2026, Mo will be releasing a multi-volume non-fiction exploration of Horror across history and cultures, **THE ANNEX OF OBSCURITIES**, also through **Tenebrous Press**.

Bri Crozier is a fine arts illustrator, comic artist, and writer best known for his award winning webcomic Blackbird Hunting. When not writing or painting, Bri can often be found looking for dead things in Kansas City.

CONTENT WARNINGS

Being a work of mature Horror, a degree of violence, gore, sex and/or death is to be expected.

In addition, ***Clairviolence*** contains

Psychological and Physical Abuse
Toxic Relationships
Child Death
Pregnancy Trauma

Please be advised.

More information at
www.tenebrouspress.com

GRAB ANOTHER TENEBROUS TITLE!

GRAB ANOTHER TENEBROUS TITLE!

TENEBROUS

PRESS

Home of New Weird Horror, New Weird Dark
Fiction, Oddities, Abnormalities and All Manner
of Eccentricities You Never Knew You Needed
More Than Oxygen

FIND OUT MORE:

www.tenebrouspress.com

@TenebrousPress on social media

HAIL THE TENEBROUS CULT

www.ingramcontent.com/pod-product-compliance
Lightning Source LLC
Chambersburg PA
CBHW031054310726
48969CB00007B/2277